HERE AND

NOW

SHERRYL D. HANCOCK

Published by Vulpine Press in the United Kingdom in 2019

ISBN 978-1-83919-283-8

Cover by Claire Wood

www.vulpine-press.com

Also in the *MidKnight Blue* series:

CHAPTER 1

The relationship between Donovan and Erin had been very sedate; they were a couple, but not really a couple. She didn't want to assume anything with him, and she knew he was basically using her to keep away the loneliness of Jeanie being gone. She also knew he needed her right now, and she figured being "used" by someone like Donovan Curtis wasn't an altogether bad thing anyway. He was very sweet, he never treated her badly—he treated her as he always had, as a friend. They hadn't actually slept together again since the first time. Erin wasn't going to push anything. She was just enjoying spending time with him when he was home, and when she could.

Donovan frequently stopped by the house she shared with two other people, asking if she wanted to do something. The day they'd gone to Joe's to check on him after the surgery, Donovan had shown up and asked if she wanted to have lunch. It was her day off from work, so she'd agreed happily, since her son was in school. When they talked it was never about Jeanie anymore. She figured if he wanted to talk about her, he would, but he never did.

On the day they found out Joe's test had come back negative, Donovan had gone searching for her to tell her the good news. He'd found her in Spider's office, oddly enough, inventorying the equipment Spider kept there.

"Hey," he said, walking in.

Erin looked up, a smudge on her pretty face. "Donovan, hi, how are you?" she asked, having not seen him for a couple of days.

Donovan leaned against Spider's desk. Spider hadn't come back down to his office from the meeting with Joe yet. "I'm good. We just found out that Joe doesn't have cancer."

"Really? That's great!" Erin said, her sincerity clear. She went to him and hugged him. "I'm really glad, Donovan."

"Yeah…" Donovan said, grinning as they parted. "I don't know if I am—I hear I was gonna be a millionaire if he died."

"Donovan!" Erin swatted him on the arm.

He laughed, then grabbed her by the waist and pulled her back to him. He was leaning against the desk with his feet planted far apart on the floor. He guided her between them, closer to him, smiling down at her.

"Think you could break away from inventory long enough to have lunch with me?" he asked, reaching a finger up to rub gently at the smudge on her cheek.

"I might be able to," she said, grinning shyly.

"Good, let's go." He glanced at his watch; it was 11:30.

"Early lunch, Sergeant?" Erin asked chidingly.

"Hey, gimme a break."

"Which arm?"

Donovan laughed, leaning down to kiss her softly on the lips. "Neither, thanks," he said quietly.

Erin was taken aback by the kiss, but enjoyed it all the same. He did sweet things like that sometimes, and it always threw her off. She was never sure what it meant, or if it meant anything. She was determined not to overthink anything he did.

He took her hand and led her out of the room. They stopped by his desk so she could put her clipboard and pen down then went out to his car. They had lunch at a local restaurant, talking about Joe's condition and what would happen now. Erin could see how much more relaxed Donovan was, and she was glad. She knew he had been very worried about his brother-in-law, and it was a huge load off his mind that Joe was going to be okay.

After an hour they went back to the department, walking into the building holding hands. That was when they ran into Jeanie, heading out of the building. All three of them stopped dead in their tracks. Jeanie stared up at Donovan, then her eyes trailed down to their hands, and then she looked at Erin, her anger becoming very evident.

"Jeanie…" Erin began.

"That didn't take long," Jeanie said.

Donovan said nothing, simply looking back at Jeanie, his face impassive.

"Jeanie, don't think that—" Erin began.

"Save it, Erin," Jeanie spat. "You got what you wanted." She said the last as her eyes went back to Donovan.

He glanced over at Erin and saw she was pale, and that was when his anger ignited.

"Who the fuck are you to talk?" he said disbelievingly.

"Excuse me?"

"About people getting what they want. I mean, you got what you wanted, right, babe? You got the job you wanted. So you should be happy, now, right?" he said, his eyes blazing at her.

"Donovan, it's not—"

"Save it," Donovan said, cutting her off. "I've heard the bullshit. But you know what? You gave me up, so don't bitch because Erin was quick to catch my fall. We all have our priorities—love just isn't one of yours."

"Oh," Jeanie replied, "and is this love *too*?" She gestured to Erin.

"It's none of your damned business what this is, Jeanie," Erin said, not wanting Donovan to have to defend himself against this. "Donovan's right—you made your own choices."

Jeanie was surprised by Erin's outburst. Apparently she'd underestimated how much Erin had wanted Donovan originally. They were both right, but that didn't make it any easier to take.

Jeanie nodded slowly, blowing her breath out in a sigh. "I'm sorry, I just—" she began, but pulled herself up short.

She wasn't going to explain to them why she was so on edge; she didn't have that luxury anymore. Once again she found herself on the wrong side of the fence. She'd long since realized that she'd blown it with Donovan, and that she'd lost him for good this time. It didn't make it any easier seeing that he'd already moved on. Nothing was going right, and she was regretting a lot of things again, but she knew it was her responsibility to get herself out of the mess she'd made.

Without a word, she stepped forward and hugged a very surprised Erin.

"Hold on to him tight," Jeanie whispered, tears in her eyes.

She reached out and touched Donovan's arm, unable to meet his eyes, then moved past them, rushing out of the building. Donovan stared after her, realizing something was very wrong but forcing himself to stay where he was. When he looked down at Erin, he saw that she had tears in her eyes. He hugged her, understanding that the confrontation had been hard on her.

He knew he was leaving Erin in limbo, not talking about the status of their relationship. He just didn't know what he wanted right then. Things were so confused. He missed Jeanie desperately. Seeing her had made his heart ache painfully. The tricks he'd picked up as a narc had come in handy to hide that ache, to keep Jeanie from seeing the damage she'd caused when she'd left. Those tricks didn't work to deny to himself that he still loved her, even when she'd kicked him in the head again. He did care about Erin, but he didn't know where a relationship with her was going to go. He didn't love her, but he enjoyed her company and wanted her close. Nothing made sense anymore, and it was driving him crazy.

Later that day, Erin went over to Donovan's house to see how he was doing. She walked in, took one look at him, and knew exactly how he was doing. And that was not well at all. He was sitting in his living room in his black leather recliner, his feet up on the matching ottoman. He was turned toward the sliding glass door that looked out toward the ocean, and the sun was just about to set. Erin also noticed the drink in his hand; she guessed correctly that this was not the first he'd had that evening. He had his Bose home theater system going, listening to music. Erin stood and watched him as one CD ended and Darren Hayes' *Spin* came on. He sang along with the first song, "Strange Relationship," with feeling, and Erin knew that was exactly how he felt at that point about the situation with Jeanie. The lyrics

5

talked about the push and pull of a relationship, how things could feel both wrong and right at the same time.

Donovan turned around as the song faded and saw Erin standing there watching him. His inner turmoil was evident on his face. She bit her lip, physically feeling the pain in his eyes. She walked toward him, getting down on her knees next to his chair. Reaching across him, she took the drink out of his hand and set it aside. She laid her hand on his cheek.

"Talk to me, Donovan," she whispered. She could see he was fairly drunk, and didn't really know if anything he would say would make sense, but she wanted to give him that chance.

"What's to talk about?" he asked, his tone dead.

"What's going on in your head," Erin supplied softly.

Donovan shrugged. "What difference does it make?"

"Come on, just talk to me, okay?" Erin said, her hand on his arm.

He looked at her hand passively, then down into her eyes. "Why do you even put up with me?"

"Because I like your cooking," Erin said, grinning. Donovan's expression didn't change. "Donovan! Look, I care about you, okay? I want you to be happy again…" She trailed off as a lump rose in her throat, tears coming to her eyes. "It makes me sick to see you so unhappy. I could just kill Jeanie for doing this to you!"

Donovan shrugged. "It's not the first time."

"Oh yeah…" Erin said, remembering what Jeanie had told her.

"Yeah, after I got shot a few years ago."

"Yeah, she told me she left you when that happened…"

Jeanie had made it sound so innocent, like it had been a mistake, but of course she'd claimed she wasn't going to do it again. Erin realized then that Jeanie had indeed repeated her mistake.

Donovan nodded in answer to her statement.

Erin got up and walked into the kitchen. She came back a minute later with the phone book in hand. She was busily flipping through the pages.

"What are you doing?" Donovan asked.

"How do you spell 'exorcist'?"

"Huh?" he said, his brows furrowing.

"Well," Erin said, tossing the book down on his lap, "I figure that what we need to do is get an exorcist to drive away the demon in you that makes you love a woman that leaves you every chance she gets." She looked at him then, canting her head to the side comically. "Think they have Jeanie-removal specialists?"

Donovan's grin was slow in coming, but then he was laughing, and Erin sensed the immediate relief of tension inside him. He grabbed her hand, pulling her down on his lap. His hand came up to pull her face down to his.

"Thank you," he said, kissing her softly on the lips.

"Any time," Erin said, smiling.

Donovan hugged her to him and she lay against him, her head on his shoulder. He moved his head so he could kiss her on the forehead a few times. They sat there together and watched the sun set, neither of them speaking. It was a very comfortable time. Erin was glad she'd been able to get him out of his slump; she knew she wouldn't always be able to, but every time she could was one less time he'd suffer. Randy was right—she loved Donovan. She wasn't sure when or how it had happened, but she loved him, and she intended to stick by him during this, even if he ended up back together with Jeanie. She also knew she'd never be able to be friends with Jeanie again, not after all that she'd seen Donovan go through because of her decision to leave.

A little while after sunset, Donovan got up to make dinner, asking her if she'd stay. Fortunately, it was one of the nights Bobby was being taken care of by her roommate. Thank God for roommates that were going for their degree in child psychology. Erin accepted his invitation gratefully.

She sat on the counter in the kitchen, watching him cook, enjoying the companionship they always shared when he did so. She'd comment on things he did, and he'd laugh and either explain or roll his eyes because she knew so little about cooking. Many times he'd turn to her and have her taste something. This evening he had her taste a sauce he was making, holding the spoon up to her lips. She told him it was great. He leaned down and kissed her for a long moment, his tongue sliding over her lips.

He stood back and nodded. "You're right, it does taste good," he said, grinning.

Erin stared back at him for a long moment, trying to regain her senses. Finally she shook her head.

"What?" he said, moving back to stir his sauce, glancing at her over his shoulder.

"You have no idea what you do, do you?"

He turned around, looking at her questioningly. "What I do, how?"

Erin hopped off the counter and walked over to him. "You can so easily take my breath away, and you don't even have to try."

Donovan looked down at her, his eyes searching hers. He reached out, cupping her face between his hands, and kissed her slowly, his lips moved over hers sensually. Erin couldn't even think. She grasped his hips, her knees going weak as he kissed her. His fingers moved through her hair, his hand sliding to the back of her head, the kiss deepening. When his tongue slipped between her lips, she moaned softly. His other hand went to the small of her back, pulling her closer to him, his lips, still kissing hers, taking on a hungry quality. She could feel his excitement as she pressed against him, and it was her undoing. She grasped at him, wanting him to make love to her.

Donovan reached back to turn off the burners on the stove, his lips never leaving hers. He backed her over to the low island, still kissing her. He pulled her blouse out of her slacks, unbuttoning it and running his hands over her skin. Following suit, Erin tugged his shirt tails out of his jeans, unbuttoning his shirt too. Before long their clothes left a trail on the floor into the living room. He made love to her on the couch, then moved to lie on his back with her lying over him, holding her.

Erin slid her hands over his arm, up to his shoulder, then to his face, touching him as if wanting to make sure he was real. He grinned up at her as she looked down at him, then turned his head to kiss her hand. They didn't talk, just lay there late into the evening. Dinner was forgotten. Erin wasn't sure what had made him react the way he had, but she definitely wasn't going to complain. She'd never had a man make love to her like Donovan did; he was gentle, but aggressive enough to keep things heated between them. She'd never had an orgasm before—her husband certainly had never taken the time to make sure she enjoyed herself. Donovan did, and Erin reveled in the difference in the experience.

***

Three days after Christian had left for San Francisco, he called Stevie in the office.

"Miss me yet?" he asked, grinning.

"No," Stevie said, grinning too.

"Uh-huh. So how's our case going?"

"It's going fine," she replied, sitting back in her chair.

"Sure you don't miss me?"

"I'm sure. When are you coming back?"

Christian laughed. "I knew you missed me."

"I do not," she said, smiling in spite of herself. "I'm just getting tired of having to handle our case all by myself, and inventory too."

"Yeah, yeah," Christian said dismissively. "A likely story. I probably won't be back for another week and a half."

Stevie sighed dramatically. "Fine, I'll just carry on with all this work then."

"They pay you."

"Oh yeah. I get patrol officer pay, woo-friggin'-hoo."

Christian laughed again. "I'll talk to you again soon. Email me if you need any help in the room—I'll try to sign on if I can."

She grinned again. "Sure, sure, have fun in San Francisco—see if I care."

"Oh, I always have fun, babe," he said, his voice lowering to a seductive drawl that made her shiver.

"Uh-huh," she said, putting her foot up on her desk and rocking in her chair in repressed agitation. "Whoring your way through the SFPD, right?"

"Of course."

Stevie dropped her foot to the floor and sat up. "Well, I better get going. The chief just walked in." No one had come into the office; she just didn't want to hear about his escapades.

"Alright, talk to you soon," he said briskly.

"Okay, bye," she said, and hung up.

Christian put down the phone, sitting back in his chair. It was the Assistant Chief's chair; she'd been watching him the whole time he'd been on the phone. She was the predatory kind—she wanted him, and she made no bones about expecting to get him. He'd put her off, telling her he was involved with someone in the department down south. He told himself that was why he'd called Stevie, not willing to admit to himself that he missed her. He was well and truly addicted to her, and he wasn't sure what he was going to do about it.

A week later, Christian lay asleep in his hotel bed. He was exhausted because he'd been working double time to get the San Francisco Police Department's system up and running. He'd been working long hours in the hopes of getting back to San Diego sooner. He'd accomplished it; he was going back in the morning, three days ahead of schedule. He'd talked to Stevie the day before at the office and she'd sounded really distant. When he'd called her at home that night, she hadn't picked up her phone. He'd even signed in to the chat room to try to talk to her, but she wasn't there. It bothered him, and it irritated him that it did. Again that night he'd tried to get ahold of her, but hadn't been able to. Once again she hadn't been in the chat room.

He was sleeping fitfully, thoughts of her in bed with someone else, like Dave Dibbins, going through his head constantly. Because his sleep was so restless he felt the soft kiss on his shoulder instantly, snapping his head around to see who had done it. He was stunned to see Stevie standing next to the bed.

Turning over and sitting up, he grabbed her around the waist, pulling her down to him and kissing her all in one fluid motion. He pressed his lips against hers deeply, hungrily devouring her as if he'd been starved for months. He pulled her closer in his intensity. Stevie kissed him back with the same fervor. As he trailed his lips down her neck, nipping at her skin, she gasped, clutching at his shoulders as her body reacted to his touch.

"Jesus, Jesus…" he chanted softly between kisses, as his fingers worked to remove the clothing between his lips and her skin.

Within minutes he was pulling her over him, moving her down his body expertly, his body sliding inside hers, making her cry out in response. She clutched at his hands as their bodies moved into a rhythm. Within minutes they were both crying out in their release. His hands slid over her skin as they lay trying to catch their breath. He pressed her against him still, not wanting to lose the contact between them. She kissed his chest. He moved his hand to caress the back of her neck through her hair as he made an "mmm" sound in the back of his throat.

After a long few minutes, Stevie raised her head to look down at him. She kissed him again. "I missed you."

He stared up into her eyes. "I missed you too."

Stevie laid her head against him again, enjoying the feeling of his hands caressing her skin, her fingers tracing patterns on his arm and chest.

"I was coming back tomorrow," he said a little while later.

"You were?" she asked, without raising her head.

Christian laughed at the tone of her voice—she sounded pretty surprised. "Yeah."

"You told me you were going to be here the full two weeks."

"Yeah, that's before I talked to you the other day."

"So?" she said, lifting her head and looking down at him.

"So, I wanted to get back. Okay?"

"Okay," she said, moving to his side, though his arm kept her close to him.

"So why did you come?" he asked, wanting to hear her say she'd missed him that much.

"I told you," she said, sounding evasive. "I missed you."

Christian turned over on his side, facing her. "Why were you so distant the other day?"

She was quiet for a moment, then shrugged. "I don't know."

"Bullshit," he replied, knowing she was evading him.

"So, why are you in bed so early?" she asked, glancing at the clock. It was only 9:30, and she'd been there over an hour now. "Don't the San Francisco cops party late?"

Christian narrowed his eyes at her. "Sure they do. But I had an early plane to catch."

"Oh."

"Are you asking if I slept with anyone here?" he asked evenly.

"No, I'm not," Stevie said, shrugging. "It's none of my business who you sleep with."

"And what about you?" he asked, his hand at her back pulling her close.

"What about me what, Collins?" she asked, lifting her head so her eyes met his in a challenge.

"Who are you sleeping with?"

"That's none of your business."

In response, he lowered his head, kissing her lips, sliding his hand down her body and caressing her skin seductively. He slipped his tongue between her lips, then pulled away only to plunge it back into her mouth erotically. Stevie groaned at her body's instant reaction. He knew exactly what to do to excite her, and he did it every time.

Within a couple of minutes, he had her clinging to him, pressing against him, wanting him again. Pulling back, he looked down into her eyes. "Who else are you sleeping with, Steve?" he asked, his tone as intense as the look in his eyes. "Tell me."

Stevie closed her eyes and shook her head, refusing to let him pull a double standard on her. Her body, on the other hand, didn't care what he pulled, as long as he touched her. His lips made a lei-surely trail down her neck, his teeth grazing her skin, making her gasp.

"Tell me," he murmured against her neck. Again she shook her head, shuddering as his fingers slid over her nipples. Her body was already betraying her, pressing to him, begging him in its own way. His hand held her back as he levered her up to slide her down his body, sliding inside her while still lying half on his side.

"Oh God…" Stevie groaned as she felt her body ready to betray her totally. "Please, please…" she said, begging her own body to listen to her for a change. Finally she gave in to what he was doing and moved to his rhythm. She cried out when he moved her off him, holding her so she couldn't pull away from him but keeping her from taking his body in hers again.

"Tell me," he said, his voice husky, his accent thick. "Who else are you sleeping with, Stevie?"

She was breathing heavily as she shook her head, his lips on her neck making her groan again as he slid her down an inch or two, her body hovering just over his.

"No one, okay, no one else," she said finally, looking down into his eyes. "Just you."

It was what he needed to hear, and he pulled her to him, kissing her deeply as he slid her down on him again. Their release was pow-erful and left them both trembling afterward. Still breathing heavily as he held her to him, his body still inside hers, Christian smiled in the half-darkness of the room. Just him. That was what he wanted to know.

The next morning Stevie woke to the feel of his lips on her neck.

Christian lay behind her, his body molded to hers, his arms wrapped around her tightly. She ran her hands over his arms, then turned over to face him. He was facing the window, so the first thing she saw was the way his light blue eyes, set against his tanned complexion, glowed in that light.

"Jesus..." she breathed, staring up at him.

He raised a jet black eyebrow at her. "What?" he asked, his accent thick because he was still drowsy.

She touched his face. "You have the most incredible eyes," she said, shaking her head as if in disbelief. "Sometimes I can't get over how handsome you are."

Christian leaned down, kissing her on the lips. "You're fairly spectacular yourself."

Stevie lowered her head, snuggling against his neck. She thought about what they'd talked about last night, and it suddenly occurred to her that he hadn't made any admissions, not like she had.

"Hey..." she said, raising her head.

"What?"

"You shit," she said, narrowing her eyes at him.

He grinned. "What did I do?"

She pinned him with a look. "Who else are you sleeping with, Collins?"

Christian laughed, turning to lie on his back, his arm keeping her close to him. "Didn't we cover this last night?"

Stevie levered herself up on her elbow. "No, Collins. I covered my sex life, not yours."

"Oh," he said simply, grinning as he glanced at her.

She jabbed him in the side with her index finger.

"Ouch!" he said, laughing all the while.

"Collins!"

"Do you want the whole list or the abridged version?" he asked, the last word raised in tone because she poked him in the ribs again.

"Collins, damnit!" she said, actually getting edgy now. Her eyes searched his.

"Well, I don't know all the names…" he began, but then caught the darkening of her eyes. He turned onto his side, reaching up to touch her face, moving closer to her. "No one else," he whispered against her lips. "Just you. Only you."

She pulled back, her eyes searching his again.

"Don't bullshit me, not now…" she said, her voice trailing off as she shook her head.

He kissed her then, sliding his hands over her skin, pulling her close, holding her to him as he moved to lie on his back. When their lips parted, she looked down at him. His eyes met hers directly.

"Why would I need anyone else when you make me feel like you do?" he asked, his voice so sincere she found it impossible to doubt him.

In response she lowered her head again, kissing him deeply, thanking him with her kiss for saying what she needed to hear. They made love that morning; it wasn't just sex this time, even though neither of them would admit it, even to themselves. Something had just changed between them with their admissions of monogamy, but they refused to examine it, for fear it would ruin it.

17

As they lay together a couple of hours later, Stevie glanced up at him, her head still against his chest. "What time is your flight this morning?"

Christian glanced at the clock, then dropped his head back on the pillow. "Two hours ago."

"Oops," Stevie said, grinning. She sat up, bringing her knees up to her chest. "So…" she began, looking down at him. "Since you've missed your flight home, what do you say to staying here a couple of days?"

Christian looked at her for a long moment, then grinned. "You're saying be like tourists or somethin'?"

"Yeah," Stevie said, shrugging. "I've never been to San Francisco."

He raised an eyebrow. "Never?"

"Nope."

He pulled her back down to him. "Then we'll have to stay a couple of days."

"I'll split the cost of the room with you."

"No, I'll pay for the room," he said, kissing her.

"Collins…"

"O'Neil…"

She grinned at him. "So what should we do today?"

"Well, take a shower to start with…"

"Which will take us another two hours," she said, grinning evilly.

Christian laughed. "At least. Then maybe we could go have

breakfast, or lunch as the case may be." His grin was mischievous, and Stevie laughed.

They took their shower, once again making love, unable to get enough of each other. Afterward Christian waited for her to get ready. He sat on the bed as she blow-dried her hair. She'd put the radio on and was moving to the music. He watched her avidly. He found that he thoroughly enjoyed the way she moved; she had an innate sensuality about her that held him captivated. She wore high-waisted shorts that made her small waist seem even smaller. On top she had only her bra, black lace. He admired her tanned and toned body. Her skin glowed with health, and he found himself wanting to touch her again.

He went to stand behind her, touching her waist, watching her eyes in the mirror, and she looked back into his. She switched the blow-dryer off, turning to face him and leaning back against the sink.

"I know what we definitely need to do while we're here," he said.

"And what's that?" she asked, her green eyes doing a lot of damage to his control.

"I want to take you out," he said, his hands still at her waist.

"Clubbing?"

"Yeah. I want to see you move like that on a dance floor."

"I didn't bring clothes for clubbing, though."

"We'll buy you something today."

"Okay…" she said, grinning. "Then we'll go clubbing."

"Good," he said, and leaned down to kiss her.

They spent the day walking along the Embarcadero, and ate lunch in Fisherman's Wharf. Stevie found herself watching him a lot as he talked to people, like vendors or other customers waiting in line. He moved and spoke with so much confidence. Stevie had always considered herself confident in herself, but Christian took it to a whole other level. There was never any hesitation in him.

She noticed more that night when they walked into a club. San Francisco had a very lively night life, and its clubs were packed with a varied type of clientele. There were people who had been going to them for years, but Christian walked in with the air of a man who owned the place. There was no doubt in his actions. He held Stevie's hand, moving through the crowd, his eyes meeting other people's directly. She found herself grinning as many a woman stood staring after him with openmouthed awe. She didn't, however, notice all the men staring at her as if they'd died and gone to heaven.

Christian was confident. He knew he looked good in all black—he always did—and he also knew without a doubt that he was with the best-looking woman in the place. The outfit they'd bought for her, chosen by Christian with her assistance, was a knock-out.

She wore a black leather mini-skirt in the softest leather that molded to her and exposed a fair amount of her legs. Her top was a spaghetti-strap, midriff-baring green-and-black print, and she wore high-heeled black ankle boots. To top the outfit off, he'd bought her a leather jacket that cut in at her waist and flared from there. She was stunned when they rang up the clothing—it had come to over $600; the jacket alone was $375. The boots had cost him another $120. Each time he'd handed the clerk his credit card without hesitation. Stevie wasn't altogether sure she liked him spending that kind of money on her, but she had to admit that he'd picked out some pretty nice stuff. When she'd dressed to go that night, she'd added her large gypsy-like gold hoop earrings, leaving her hair loose and tousled-looking.

Christian had been satisfactorily awed by her appearance. They almost hadn't made it out of the room, since she was just as impressed by his. In fact, when she'd first seen him wearing his black slacks, belt, and boots, with no shirt since he was shaving, she'd walked up behind him, sliding her hands up his chest, enjoying his sharp intake of breath at the feel of her nails on his skin. He'd finished shaving and turned to her, pulling her close and kissing her deeply.

It had taken everything she had to pull away and tell him they needed to get going if they ever hoped to find a table at any club in the city. She'd gone down to the front desk to ask for suggestions as to which club to go to. The concierge had been clueless; it was the bellhops, younger guys who had been eyeing Stevie since the moment she'd walked up, that helped her out, telling her about all the best places in the area and which ones to avoid. Stevie had thanked them both with a wink.

Now that they had arrived, Christian had taken over. He found them a table amidst the other patrons. The waitress came over immediately, having tracked their progress through the club. She spoke to Christian, ignoring Stevie.

"Can I get you something?" she asked, her look telling him he could have anything he wanted.

Christian raised an eyebrow at the woman, not surprised by the not-so-subtle come-on. He glanced over at Stevie, who was grinning at him. "What do you want, babe?" he asked, purposely using the familiar term.

"What are you having?"

"A shot and a beer."

"That works," Stevie said, surprising him.

He nodded, looking impressed, then turned back to the waitress. "Two shots of Herradura and two Coronas."

The waitress nodded and walked away.

"You drink tequila, huh?" he asked Stevie.

Stevie grinned. "Yep." She shrugged off her jacket, and Christian could almost feel every guy in the place sigh. "What?" Stevie asked, catching his grin.

He shook his head, looking around. He'd been right; there were at least ten guys watching her with very definite interest. It was going to be an interesting night.

When their order arrived, Christian tossed down a twenty and a five for a twenty-dollar tab. The waitress smiled at him, giving him a wink. They drank their shots, and Christian was happy to note that Stevie didn't even wince. She did indeed drink tequila; she hadn't been trying to impress him.

Toya's song "I Do!!" came on, and Stevie grabbed Christian's hand. "We need to dance."

Christian got up, and she pulled him to the dance floor, her body already moving to the music. She found that he did indeed know how to move, but she was the main one dancing, his hands at her hips as she moved with him, her arms up over her head.

"This song is so you," she said, practically yelling so he could hear her. Then she started singing the words to him. They talked about him being an all-out "baller" with the ladies and how they all wanted him.

As the song played on, Christian slid his hands up to bare skin, pulling Stevie close and kissing her. He moved his lips to her ear.

"And you know they all want you too, don't you?"

She looked up at him and smiled brilliantly. "But all I want is you."

"Oh, you got me, babe, trust me."

They danced for a while, then went back to their table. A guy stopped Stevie before she sat down, asking her to dance. She looked over at Christian; he shrugged and nodded, so she said yes. Christian ordered two more shots from the waitress and watched Stevie on the dance floor. The guy she was with couldn't come close to keeping up with her, but he tried. When that song ended, another guy grabbed Stevie; she glanced over at Christian, and he held up a shot to her and drank it. She laughed, watching him even as she started to dance. This happened a few times, to the point that he drank her shot and ordered two more for himself.

Stevie was enjoying herself. She didn't give one care about the guys she was dancing with, her eyes constantly trailing over to Christian. She could see women watching him too, but none of them seemed to be able to work up the courage to approach him. He sat with his legs extended in front of him, crossed at the ankles. He held a bottle of beer in his hand and looked at home for all intents and purposes. And he was watching her. And it was him she was dancing for.

When the DJ started mixing in a slow song, the guy she was dancing with seemed to be under the impression she would be all too happy to dance slow with him too. Before she had a chance to tell him she wasn't interested, Christian was there.

"I'll take over now," he told the other man.

"Bullshit," the younger guy said, grabbing at Stevie.

"Remove your hands, or I'll remove them for you. She's with me," Christian said, his voice very serious.

"Fuck you."

Without a word Christian reached out and grabbed him by a handful of his shirt, lowering his face to the shorter man's. "I said, she's with me," he growled, his voice thick with menace. The man's friends saw fit to pull him away then, seeing that Christian wasn't quite the pushover pretty boy the younger man had taken him for.

As if nothing had happened, Christian turned back to Stevie and pulled her close as the song started.

"You okay?" he asked.

"With you here," Stevie said, moving closer to him, "of course I am."

They danced to the song "Insatiable," both listening to the words and both thinking the same thing—that was what they were. The lyrics talked about making love till all hours of the night and thoroughly enjoying themselves—and how their love for each other was insatiable.

When the song faded, Christian kissed her deeply, making it very evident to anyone paying even the slightest attention that she was very definitely his lady.

After that, no one dared to ask her to dance again, though she finally joined up with a few of the ladies dancing together. They all asked her about Christian, and she told them that yes, she was seeing him, but they were more than welcome to make a play for him if they wanted to. None of them tried; it was pretty obvious from the way he watched Stevie that he wasn't interested in anyone but her. Stevie found that she liked that a lot. She and Christian danced together a few more times too, and every time, she found that she enjoyed the way he moved. He was very sensual, never more than an inch from her, his body moving with hers. He reminded her of the men that did salsa dancing; he had a very natural rhythm, but didn't make any attempt to dance like a lot of the guys were doing. He moved to the music while letting her do all the actual dancing, his hands always touching her, either at the waist or on the hips.

They were sitting at the table when a dark-haired woman walked up behind Christian and threw her arms around him, then kissed him on the cheek. He looked back, surprised, but then turned and stood, grabbing her up in a hug.

"I knew it was you!" the woman said. "What are you doing here?"

"Working. You?" Christian said as he set her down on her feet.

She grinned. "Working too."

"Oh, hey," Christian said, turning to Stevie. "Steve, this is Jeanie Franco. Jeanie, this is Stevie O'Neil."

Jeanie stepped forward, extending her hand. Stevie shook it, thinking she'd heard that name somewhere.

"Jeanie used to work at the PD," Christian supplied, seeing Stevie's mind working.

"Oh, yeah, okay," Stevie said, smiling.

"So, you're on the job?" Christian said, giving Jeanie a once-over look then raising a jet black eyebrow.

"You expect me to come in here in uniform, dummy?" Jeanie countered, grinning at him.

He laughed. "Yeah, with 'cop' tattooed on your forehead."

"Can I steal you for a dance?" Jeanie asked, then looked over at Stevie.

Stevie shrugged. Christian took Jeanie's hand and led her to the floor. Shortly after, the song changed to a slow dance. Stevie watched as they moved together, knowing without a doubt that he'd slept with Jeanie before. She could tell by the comfortable way they moved together. There was no hesitation or unfamiliarity. She saw Jeanie smiling and laughing a few times, shaking her head. Stevie felt her stomach tighten with jealousy, a feeling she was fairly unaccustomed to.

She looked for the waitress, but she was nowhere in sight. Reaching into her jacket pocket, Stevie pulled out a twenty-dollar bill and headed to the bar. When she got there she ordered a double shot of Herradura, drank it down, and ordered another. Throwing down the twenty, she turned around, searching the dance floor for Christian. She tossed the shot back and set the glass on the bar.

"Can I buy you another one?" asked a man standing next to her. He was tall, Hispanic, decent-looking. She shrugged, nodding.

He bought her a drink and one for himself. They drank the shots together. The tequila was catching up with her now; she could feel her buzz turning into a deeper, more numb feeling. She shook her head to try and clear it a bit.

"You okay?" the guy asked, eyeing her.

"Yeah, I'm good. I'm okay," she said, and started to head back to her table.

"Hey, where you going?" he asked, his hand on her arm stopping her.

Stevie turned back to him. "Let go of me," she said evenly.

"Hey, babe, try being nice," the man said, seemingly feeling pretty full of himself.

"I am being nice. I haven't decked your ass yet."

The guy laughed, apparently thinking she was kidding. He tightened his grip on her arm, pulling her back toward him. Without warning she balled her fist and threw a punch worthy of a prize fighter. The man staggered back, his hand going to his jaw. His eyes narrowed. "You fucking bitch…" he muttered. Everyone around them was laughing at him. He clenched his fist, but Stevie didn't back down, her head coming up as she waited for him to try something.

"What are you doing?" Christian said from behind her, which made her turn around.

She didn't see the guy coming at her then, but Christian did, and he pushed her aside, throwing a punch that laid him out flat on the ground.

Stevie turned back to look at the guy on the floor. Then she looked at Christian; he was watching her, still waiting for an answer to his question.

"I was mingling," she said sweetly.

His slow smile started then, and eventually he was laughing as he pulled her to him, hugging her. "Can't take you anywhere."

"You either," she said, taking his hand and examining the cut on his knuckle. She kissed his hand and led him back to the table.

"You throw a pretty mean punch, O'Neil," he said over another beer.

"You too, Collins," she countered, smiling at him.

It was indeed an interesting evening.

CHAPTER 2

Dave lay asleep. He'd come home from his undercover work, taken a shower, and gone to bed. He rarely slept much when he was undercover, grabbing an hour here or there. There was always some kind of party he had to be at, or a late-night meeting. Even when he did get back to the sleazy apartment he used, he could never sleep; he was constantly on his guard, and never felt relaxed enough. So when he got home, he was always beyond exhausted. It was common for him to sleep for twenty-four hours when he got back.

The morning after he'd gotten in, Stevie walked into his room.

"You are back," she said, having just gotten home from San Francisco with Christian the night before.

Dave turned over tiredly, looking at her through barely open eyes. "Yeah, I'm back."

Stevie sat down on the bed. "You look like crap, hon."

"Thanks," he said, grinning as he rubbed his eyes. "What's up with you?"

Stevie shrugged, but she was grinning too, and Dave knew she wanted to talk to him about something.

"Come on, Steve, what's up?" Dave sat up. He wore gray sweatpants and no shirt.

"Nothing major," she said, shaking her head. "Just got back

from San Francisco."

"What were you doing there?"

"I went up there to, um…"

"To what?"

"To see Christian," she said, giving him a sidelong glance.

Dave nodded. "Why was he up there?"

"Working on their computers at the PD."

"Uh-huh…" Dave said, waiting for the rest of the story.

Stevie grinned. "Don't start with me, Dibbins, okay?"

He narrowed his eyes at her, as if visually gleaning more information than she was giving, and in fact he was. She was glowing; he could tell she was falling hard for Christian Collins. It surprised him—he had taken her for a hardcore player too. Now she was falling for a major player.

"Just be careful, Steve."

"Yeah, yeah, I know. I'm cool, it's okay." She moved to lie down across the foot of the bed, propping herself up on her elbow. "I'm just having fun," she said. "So what's this I hear about you and Susan?"

Dave looked at her for a long moment, narrowing his eyes at her. Christian had obviously told her about Susan, so Susan must have told Christian. Great, the whole world knew. He shrugged. "We went out. Why?"

Stevie didn't reply, turning to lie on her back. "She's not like us, Dave… and she's definitely not someone to mess with if you're just playing."

Dave looked back at her for a long moment, then shook his

head. "I know all about her, okay? It's cool."

"Dave, her uncle will kill you," Stevie said, sitting up in her sudden desire to make him understand. She'd had a long discussion about Susan with Christian. He'd told her about the time Rick had found out he was sleeping with Susan; Rick had gone after Christian, but even then, Christian was Joe's cousin. Dave was no relation at all. She honestly believed Rick Debenshire would beat the shit out of Dave if he toyed with Susan Endicott.

"Stevie, stay out of it," Dave said, losing his patience. He was already in enough turmoil over what to do about Susan; he didn't need Stevie telling him what he should do too.

Stevie stared at him for a minute, then shook her head. "It's your head, not mine."

"That's right," Dave said. "You know, you're the one sleeping with the guy she's in love with…" he said, feeling the need to remove some of the blame from himself.

Stevie narrowed her eyes at him. "Low blow," she said simply. She got up and walked out.

Dave sighed to himself. Now he was running his friends off. What next?

What was next was Susan showing up at his house a couple of hours later. She had heard from Christian that Dave was back. She wanted to know what was going to happen with them, and she wanted to know right now.

"David, it's me," she said into the intercom.

Dave sighed, pushing the button to let her into the house. She walked into his bedroom a few minutes later, and noted how tired he looked as he sat up. She also noticed the remnants of a bruise and a cut on his jaw.

"I heard you were back," she said quietly.

Dave nodded, then took a deep breath. "Look, we need to talk."

"Alright," she said, sitting on the bed, but not close to him. He could tell she already knew what was coming, and it bothered him.

He looked at her for a long moment, his face drawn and unhappy. "I can't see you anymore," he said simply. Susan nodded, her lips trembling slightly. "I can't explain it right now," he continued, feeling like a royal asshole. "I just... I need to keep things simple, okay?"

Again she nodded, pressing her lips together as if to keep from saying something. Which was true—she didn't want to make a fool out of herself by begging him not to do this.

"Susan?" Dave said when she made no comment. His blue eyes watched her, trying to discern if she was okay or not.

"I understand," she said finally, sounding like she felt anything but understanding. With that she stood up, averting her eyes from him.

"Take care," she said, then turned and walked out of the room.

Dave closed his eyes, having to wrestle with himself mentally to keep from running after her. He banged his head against the wall a few times, feeling absolutely sick at what he'd just done. But he'd decided this was for the best.

For one thing, she was affecting his work; he couldn't concentrate when thoughts of her kept popping up in his mind. He knew that being distracted could get him killed, and dead was for a very long time. He also realized there was no way anything could work with her; he was old enough to be her father, and they were worlds apart, socially, economically, and very definitely chronologically. It wouldn't work, and there was no sense in leading her on any more than he already had. It was crazy. He hated himself for hurting her, but he figured it was better to break it off now before she really got hurt.

Susan was at the department an hour later. Joe had called her to ask her to bring his prescription to the office; he'd forgotten it, and Randy was in class. Susan tried not to think about what had happened at Dave's house. She had felt thrown out with the trash. He had played with her and was now apparently done with her. It made her sick to realize that she'd pinned her heart on a man that had done that to her.

As she wandered down the hallway after dropping the medicine off with Joe, she found herself at a familiar door. It was the one to the office Christian shared with Rhiannon Templeton. She'd been there often enough while they were dating. Without stopping to think, she opened the door and walked in. Christian was working at his computer, with Stevie sat at the desk, calling out numbers to him. Christian looked up and saw Susan's despair immediately.

"Zan, what's wrong?" he asked, reverting to the nickname he'd given her when they were together. He stood up, touching her shoulder.

She shook her head miserably. He immediately pulled her into his arms, and Susan leaned against him gratefully. Stevie turned around, watching.

"Come on, babe, what's wrong?" Christian asked softly.

"I'm a stupid fool, that's what," Susan said, near tears again.

Christian glanced over at Stevie. She looked down, shaking her head. She knew Christian had told Susan that Dave was back, and she was fairly sure Dave had just broken it off with her. Glancing at her watch, Stevie made a quick decision. She stood up, pulling her jacket on.

"I think Susan and I need to have lunch," she said, giving Christian a pointed look.

He looked worried suddenly. Susan looked up at her, confusion clear on her face.

"You have time?" Stevie asked.

"Sure…" Susan said.

"Come on," Stevie said, and gestured for Susan to precede her.

Susan wiped at her eyes, then turned and walked out, glancing back at Christian. He shrugged, giving Stevie a bewildered look. She just looked back at him for a long moment, then quirked her lips in a quick grin before following Susan out of the office.

Stevie led Susan to her green Trans Am. Unlocking the doors with her remote, she gestured for her to get in. Stevie got in on the driver's side, putting the key in the ignition and starting the car with a satisfying rumble. She reached over and pushed in a CD as she backed out of the space. She pressed the forward button to skip through the tracks, stopping at the one she obviously wanted. Stevie had bought Darren Hayes' CD, having liked the song "Insatiable." She'd found another song on the album that she really liked, called "Dirty." She put the track on, singing along as Susan watched her, listening to the words too. The song started off with two people who were obviously caught up in a moment of passion, then followed with

33

Darren Hayes saying "Oh… ooohhh ohh… yeah, yeah, yeah!" in a very sexy way. Stevie sang right along with it, her rich auburn hair blowing in the breeze as she opened the windows. When the words started again, Susan looked over at Stevie and wondered if they matched the woman singing them. She knew Christian was seeing her, and she could also tell from the way Stevie carried herself that she was a good match in confidence for someone like Christian. Stevie wasn't shy at all, and she had the looks to carry off the confidence she exuded.

As the song faded, Stevie reached over and turned down the radio. She was speeding down the road, weaving in and out of traffic smoothly.

"So what's going on with you and Dave?" she asked without preamble.

"I…" Susan stammered, not sure what to say. Knowing that Stevie had been dating Dave, and was now seeing Christian, she wasn't sure what she *could* say to the woman.

"Look," Stevie said, giving her a direct look at the next red light, "Dave and I were seeing each other for a bit, but we're friends now—no big deal. You can talk without worrying about offending me."

Susan nodded, not sure how Stevie could think the way she did. Apparently what she was thinking showed on her face, because Stevie shook her head and said, "I know it's probably impossible for someone like you to understand, but I don't have to love the guys I sleep with. It's just casual to me. But I know you're not like that, and I know you were seeing Dave. So what happened?"

Susan hesitated for a moment longer, but in truth she did like

Stevie; from what little she had seen, she was a lot like her aunt Midnight. Stevie was independent, but she had been the one who had told Susan not to wait around for Christian, that no man was worth that. She decided then that perhaps, like Midnight, Stevie O'Neil might just be the person to get advice on men from.

"I seem to have a problem with choosing the wrong men," Susan said, sighing.

Stevie glanced at her. "Okay…"

"Well, you know I couldn't get Christian to commit to me, even though he claims to love me."

"He does love you," Stevie put in.

"How do you know?" Susan asked, surprised by Stevie's words.

Stevie shrugged. "He told me."

Susan looked back at her for a long moment, stunned by the admission. She shook her head in disbelief. Christian had told the woman he was sleeping with that he was in love with another woman?

"He never ceases to amaze me," Susan said, rolling her eyes. "He's so bloody insensitive sometimes."

Stevie shrugged. "Guys like Christian are actually what I prefer. I want a guy to be upfront with me—I don't like games. He loves you. He cares about you deeply, he just has a hard time with commitment."

"And I bore him," Susan said wisely.

Stevie didn't respond to that, not wanting to hurt her. She knew that was part of the problem with Susan and Christian, but there was more to it than that, and now was not the time to go into it. Susan caught the silence, and knew that she was right. She'd always known that, though; Christian needed much more in a woman than Susan could ever be, and she'd come to accept that.

"So what happened with Dave?" Stevie asked, trying to get the conversation back on track.

"Well... I'm not sure, really..." Susan said. "Things were fine before he left. We went out on a date, he was very nice, charming..."

"Good in bed," Stevie put in, grinning devilishly.

Susan laughed at that bold admission, but nodded, even as the blush crept up her cheeks.

"So what happened between then and now?" Stevie asked.

"Well, about three days after he left to go back to work, he called me late one night."

"He called you?" Stevie asked, surprised.

"Yes, he said he just wanted to hear my voice." Susan smiled again as she remembered how he had said it.

"Okay, then what happened?"

"Well, he got really quiet, and then said he needed to get off the phone," Susan said, her confusion at Dave's change in moods evident.

Stevie nodded. "Was he calling on a cell phone?"

"Yes, I believe so."

"Okay, cells are easy to trace, and it was pretty dangerous for him to call you at all."

"It was?" Susan was aghast that he'd put himself in some kind of danger.

"Yeah, if he's undercover—and I know he does deep cover—he leaves behind his whole life when he goes. He has no connection with his real life." Stevie looked over at Susan. "If he called you, it means you were in his head, and he wanted to make a connection with you."

Susan wasn't sure what to say. "But he just told me he can't see me anymore," she said eventually.

"He did?"

"Yes."

Stevie parked in the nearest lot and sat back to think. "He just broke it off this morning?"

"Yes, when I went over there."

"Did he seem okay with doing that?"

"What, breaking up with me?"

"Yeah."

"Well, no, he didn't seem very happy. I just assumed it was because I had come to his house without him asking me to."

Stevie pursed her lips. She knew what was going on, or was fairly sure she did, but wasn't sure if she should tell Susan what she was thinking.

"Look, Susan," she began, turning to face the other woman. "Dave's a very high-level player. He's used to controlling everything that goes on in his love life. He's got everything the way he likes it." Stevie narrowed her eyes then. "But you're messing up that equation somehow... and I think that's why he broke it off."

"Messing with it how? What have I done?" Susan asked, bewildered.

Stevie smiled. "You're getting to him."

"In a bad way?"

Stevie shrugged. "Well, yeah, for him it's a bad way—he doesn't know how to handle it."

Susan looked supremely confused, so Stevie explained. "Look, in the work Dave does, he needs to keep himself under control at all times. He needs to control his reactions, his heart, his mind—everything. And if he's got you in his head, and he can't get you out, he figures the only way to remedy that is to stop seeing you."

"So what do I do?" Susan asked.

"Do you want him?"

"Yes," Susan answered without reserve.

Stevie narrowed her eyes at the other woman. "You're falling for him, aren't you?"

Susan bit her lower lip, lowering her eyes, then nodded miserably.

Stevie nodded. "Then I'm telling you here and now, you need to go after him."

"Are you crazy?" Susan said, her eyes wide. "He just told me he doesn't want to see me!"

Stevie pinned her with a look. "Do you want him, Susan?"

"Yes, but—"

"No buts. If you want him, you need to take the initiative here. Go to him, tell him you want him—hell, tell him you're in love with him, because God knows you are. Let the chips fall where they may."

Susan's eyes widened, and she bit her lip again. "What if he tells me to go away?"

Stevie shrugged. "Then you're not out anything more than you were before, right? You're not getting to be with him right now, are you?"

"I don't know…" Susan said, shaking her head. "I don't think I can do this…"

Stevie shrugged. "Well, you can just accept his decision and live with it…" She looked directly into Susan's eyes. "But that's what you did with Christian, and look where that got you."

Susan looked back at Stevie for a long moment, stunned by her comment, which on the surface seemed mean-spirited. But then she thought about it, and it was true. She had accepted Christian's treatment of her, his sleeping around and telling her that he couldn't commit. She'd done it thinking it would at least keep him around, but what had it gotten her? Nothing.

Stevie started the car up again and pulled out of the lot. As she drove toward Sea Port Village, they pulled up to a light. A black car came up next to them. Neither Stevie nor Susan was paying attention to the vehicle when the man inside it honked his horn. Stevie glanced over, as did Susan. Stevie gave the car an assessing look, from the nose to the rear, then nodded to the driver. The guy, a black man with a blue bandana around his forehead, revved his engine. Stevie just shook her head, grinning, and turned back to the light. Susan glanced over at Stevie and had time to say "You're not—" before the light changed and Stevie threw the Trans Am into gear and took off. The Camaro took off right after them. The race was on.

There was a fairly long stretch of road, which was thankfully clear at that moment. Stevie's engine roared with power as she threw it into fourth gear. The Camaro was keeping up right up until that point, then Stevie put her foot down and shot ahead, beating the light they'd been approaching.

"Yes!" Stevie crowed as she slowed her car down.

The Camaro caught up to them at the next light. Stevie pushed the button to put Susan's window down, leaning forward to catch the young man's look.

"*Dayam*, girl!" he said, laughing.

"You got just as many horses under that hood as I do, bro—I just know how to run mine," she said, winking. The light changed then, and they left the Camaro behind with the driver still laughing and shaking his head.

Susan looked at Stevie for a long moment. "You enjoyed that, didn't you?"

"Oh yeah," Stevie said, smiling. "I love putting men in the basement when it comes to speed."

Susan shook her head, laughing softly. Stevie was definitely a wild one.

When they reached Sea Port Village, they went to lunch at the People's Fish Market, a little sidewalk place. They got their food and sat outside.

"So what are you going to do?" Stevie asked, picking up a French fry and eating it, her fiery hair glistening in the sun and blowing in the breeze.

Men walking by stopped to look at her. She was wearing jeans with a black tank top and black boots, her hair was loose, and she wore the gold hoop earrings she always favored. She looked like a gypsy. Sunglasses covered her emerald green eyes, but it was obvious she had a very pretty face, with high cheekbones and smooth, tanned skin. Stevie didn't pay any attention to the men who stopped to gape at her.

"Susan?" she prompted when the other woman didn't answer.

"I'm sorry," Susan said, smiling. "I was just thinking…" she began, then shook her head. "Anyway, I don't know what I'm going to do about David, but you're right—if I just let him go, then it's my own fault."

"Susan, you can't always get something you want by waiting around for it. Sometimes you have to go and grab it."

"Is that what you did?" Susan asked, picking up her iced tea and taking a sip.

"What I did about what?" Stevie asked, her brows furrowing.

"With Christian."

"Susan…" Stevie began, not sure if the girl was going to nail her now for sleeping with Christian or what.

"No, don't worry," Susan said, waving away Stevie's obvious hesitation. "I understand that Christian needs someone like you."

"Like me?" Stevie repeated, not altogether sure she liked the term there.

"I mean, someone wild like him."

Stevie grinned, thinking Susan was a lot more insightful than anyone gave her credit for. "And you've decided I'm wild?"

"Aren't you?"

"I'm a bit of a wild child, yeah," Stevie said, laughing.

"You are much more Christian's style than I ever was," Susan said, her tone not indicating any kind of rancor at the admission.

"Well, he and I are both players. That doesn't usually make for heavy romance, but it's fun while it lasts." Stevie shrugged at the last part.

Susan looked at her for a long moment, as if assessing her statement. "I think you two might be better suited than for something casual."

Stevie shrugged, looking over her shoulder at the bay, avoiding talking about the point. She didn't want to pursue this conversation any further. Susan stayed quiet; she could tell the subject was sensitive, and just as Stevie had discerned about her feelings for Dave, Susan could tell Stevie felt a lot more for Christian than she wanted to admit, maybe even to herself.

They talked about other things as they finished lunch. They discussed Joe's diagnosis and what a relief it was. Stevie took Susan back to her car, and Susan got out, bending down to look through the driver's window.

"Thank you for this," she said, smiling.

Stevie grinned. "I'm a sucker for a happy ending. Just go after him, Susan. You don't lose anything for trying, and you could gain one helluva guy for yourself."

Susan smiled and nodded. "We'll see what courage I can muster."

"Don't think about it—just do it."

Susan nodded again, then waved. Stevie drove back to the regular lot and parked. She went inside and back to the office space she was sharing with Christian.

"And what did I miss?" he asked when she walked in.

"A lot of girl talk, nothing you could handle," Stevie said, tossing her keys on the desk.

"Uh-huh," he said, watching her eyes.

"It wasn't about you."

"Why not?" he asked, grinning.

"Not everything is about you, Collins!" she said, laughing as she swatted him on the head.

"Seriously, though, is she okay?"

Stevie looked thoughtful for a moment, then nodded. "I think she will be if she just does what she needs to."

"And what is that?"

"Don't worry about it."

Stevie wasn't willing to tell him what she and Susan had talked about, at least not until she knew if it had worked. She wasn't sure if Christian would be too happy with her for telling Susan to go for Dave. She was half afraid that Christian would think she was trying to run Susan off so she could keep him for herself. That wasn't her style; if she had competition she met it head on, not with sneaky back-door tactics. She knew Susan and Christian weren't ever going to make it, just from what he'd told her and from what Susan herself had said.

But Susan might just be what Dave needed to settle down, and Stevie wanted the best for her friend. Dave had plenty of excitement in his life at work; he needed someone stable and gentle to come home to. Who better than an English nanny? Couldn't get much more stable and gentle than that. She hoped she'd done the right thing. But what she had said was true—Susan would lose nothing by confronting Dave about breaking it off with her.

***

Erin was sitting at her desk, typing a document for one of the lieutenants, when her phone rang. "Erin Shandley."

"Your name is Bodine, Erin," said a menacingly familiar voice.

Erin gasped. "Tyler?" she breathed, her heart beating a mile a minute.

"Oh, you remember me now, huh? You little bitch, how dare you take my son!"

"Tyler, wh-where are you?" Erin asked, stuttering in her effort to control her trembling.

"You don't worry where I am, you little whore. You'll see me soon enough, and you'll pay for taking off like that. No one takes my kid and my money and leaves me." With that he hung up.

Erin put the receiver down, her hands shaking badly. She tried to calm down, but was having a hard time breathing. Donovan walked up just then.

"Erin?" he said, seeing that she was pale. "Are you okay?" He knelt down next to her desk, taking her hands in his and looking up at her. "Erin?"

"Donovan…" she began, but she was too shaken up to explain.

"Come on," he said, standing and pulling her up from her chair.

He walked her outside and across the street to the coffee shop. They went inside and he ordered for both of them, then found them a table in the corner where it was quiet.

"Okay, tell me what's going on," he said.

Erin told him everything about her marriage to Tyler. She started with how they'd met and how she'd gotten pregnant, then told him about the abuse and how she'd taken it until Tyler had hit Bobby.

"Then I had to go. I knew it would only get worse from there," she said, tears still drying on her cheeks.

Donovan brushed at her tears with his thumb. "You're right, Erin—you were right to leave," he said, his eyes somber.

"But now he's found me," she said, finally getting to today's occurrence. "He called me at work."

"He called you? How did he find you?"

"I don't know, but he did… and I don't know what to do," she said, tears coming to her eyes again. "What if he takes Bobby? What if he… God, I don't know."

Donovan nodded. "Okay, okay, let's take this one step at a time. If he knows where you work, then he could possibly know where you live. Maybe not, but let's be safe about this."

"What can I do? I don't have the money to move," she said, shaking her head.

"I know, so you and Bobby will move in with me till we find Tyler."

"Donovan, we can't do that…"

"Why not?"

"You can barely handle having your niece and nephew over for a few hours—you have no idea what it's like to live with a five-year-old twenty-four-seven. I couldn't possibly do that to you."

"I'm not asking you, Erin," Donovan said, taking her hand. "I'm telling you, this is what we're doing. I'm not taking any chances with your safety. This guy is mad, and he's going to cause you trouble if you aren't careful."

Erin nodded slowly. "But it's so much on you…" Her voice trailed off as she looked down at her hands.

"Hey," he said, touching her under the chin to lift her eyes to his. "You've done a lot for me, gotten me through a lot of crap lately. It's my turn to do something for you, okay?"

Erin bit her lip, looking very unsure. Donovan leaned forward, kissing her softly. "No more arguing—we'll take care of it tonight. Till then, don't answer your phone—let the voicemail get it, okay?"

"Okay," Erin said, finally starting to feel better. She hadn't expected Donovan to help her like this. She'd never dreamed he'd ask her to move in with him to help her out. When they stood up to leave, she hugged him. "Thank you, Donovan. Thank you so much."

"That's what friends are for, right?" he said, smiling down at her.

"I think this is above and beyond that."

He shrugged. "You've been there for me, Erin. It's my turn."

He walked her back to her office, kissing her softly on the lips at her desk, then turned and left to go back up to his area. The girls in the secretary pool all whispered about the handsome narc Erin was seeing, the one that used to be engaged to another officer in the department. Erin ignored all the looks and whispering. She did as Donovan had told her, and didn't answer her phone when it rang. Tyler, however, didn't call back that day.

It was nine o'clock at night when Susan finally made the decision to go and talk to Dave. She drove over to his house and walked up to the front door. She buzzed the intercom and waited. There was no answer. She buzzed again, and wondered if perhaps he'd left. She went over to the garage and, peeking in the window, saw his Charger there. He was definitely home. Maybe he was avoiding her. Susan walked back to the door and buzzed a few more times. Once again indecision set in, but then anger took over; she had a right to know why he'd broken it off with her, and she was going to find out.

Punching in the code she'd learned while helping him with his back, she walked inside. The house was dark and quiet. She turned on the light in the living room; it was empty.

"David?" she called out, not wanting to surprise him.

There was no answer. She walked down the hallway to his bedroom. She saw him lying on the bed on his side. The light in the bathroom was on so she could see his face; he looked like he was sleeping.

"David?" she said, raising her voice a bit.

He stirred and opened his eyes slightly.

She crossed over to the bed. "David," she said, louder this time. He stirred again, then groaned as he glanced up at her.

"What are you doin' here?" he said, his words slurred.

Susan stared down at him. "David, what's wrong with you?"

He looked back at her blearily for a long moment, then raised his hand, pointing at his dresser. On the top of it stood an empty fifth of Jack Daniels.

"Oh lord," Susan said, shaking her head. "How much of that did you have to drink?"

"All of it," he said, turning over on his stomach and pushing the pillows out of the way, curving his arm around in front of his face.

"Oh, David..." Susan said, moving to kneel next to the bed, reaching out to brush his hair back from his face. "Why?"

Dave was quiet for a few moments, then opened one blue eye and looked at her. "Do you have any idea what kind of garbage I deal with? The scum of the earth, the people no one wants..." His words were muffled by his arm and slurred from the alcohol in his veins. Susan was silent, letting him say his piece. "These people are scum. They're scum, and all of a sudden they have money because they sold dope to some third-grader... and they suddenly think they're gods. They think they can do anything and no one can touch them. They're crap, excrement, and I have to play one of them every day..." He trailed off as he scrubbed at his face with his hand. "Then there's you..." he said, his voice softening. "And you're so nice and sweet and just... so... so..." he stammered, closing his eyes and rubbing his face on the bed.

"So what, David?" Susan asked when it was apparent he wasn't going to finish.

Again he was silent. He looked at her for a long moment, then reached out and touched her cheek. "God, you're beautiful."

Susan smiled softly at him. "I'm so what, David?"

He looked at her for a minute, then blew his breath out in a sigh. "So beyond me," he said. "You don't know these people. The depths they sink to, the way their minds think, they just… and I can't, I just… I can't. You're not, you… and I can't… with you, I just—"

"David," Susan said, trying to stop him.

"Susan, I can't, I just can't… you're not…" he began again, struggling to make sense.

"David, I love you," she said in a rush.

"I can't—You what?"

"I said I love you, David."

Dave swallowed a few times, moving slowly to sit up. Susan stood as he did. He stared at her openmouthed for a long moment. "You… love me?"

"Yes," Susan said, smiling at him.

"Are you sure?" he asked, his eyes searching hers.

"David!" she exclaimed, sitting down on the bed. "Yes, I'm sure."

"This is the old narc you're talking about… right?" he said, a slow grin starting on his lips. His words were still a little slurred, but he had definitely sobered up a bit with her admission.

"You are not old!" she said, giving him a stern look.

"Honey, I'm sixteen years older than you."

"I don't care," she said, reaching out to touch his lips when he started to say something else. "I love you."

His eyes searched hers again for a long moment. Then he reached up, touching her cheek, smoothing his thumb over it, then slid his hand to the back of her head, pulling her to him. His lips met hers, kissing her softly, repeatedly. His arms encircled her, holding her to him, then he pulled back to look down at her. She gazed back at him, her eyes searching his face.

"I went to my car while I was undercover," he said, "and I got my jacket out, and when I put it on, it still had your perfume on it... I was lost. All I wanted to do was come home. That's never happened to me before. I tried to get you out of my head, but I couldn't—that's why I called you..."

"And that was dangerous for you," Susan said, remembering what Stevie had told her.

He looked surprised that she knew that, then nodded. "Yeah, it is... but I just wanted to hear you... to feel you close to me one more time." He kissed her again. "And I knew... I knew..."

"What did you know?" Susan asked, holding her breath.

"That I love you," he said, staring down into her eyes.

She smiled brilliantly at him. He'd said just what she'd hoped to hear. He kissed her deeply, pulling her closer, caressing her back. Moving back again, he looked down at her. "I'm gonna be pretty pissed off if I wake up in the morning and find out this was all a drunken hallucination, you know."

Susan laughed. "You're not hallucinating," she said, placing her hand on his cheek. "I love you."

"Good," he said, leaning in to take possession of her lips again.

He took his time removing her clothes, kissing her and caressing her all the while. When he made love to her it was with the utmost care, taking it slow and savoring every moment.

Afterward, she lay in his arms, feeling happy and at peace. When she looked over at him, she saw that he was staring down at her.

"You owe me, you know," she said.

He grinned. "I know."

"For the…" She leaned up to look at the clock on his nightstand. "Ten hours and twenty-five minutes of misery you put me through today."

"What made you come back?"

"Stevie," Susan answered simply.

"Stevie made you come back?" he asked, bewildered.

"Yes. She told me that if I truly wanted you, I shouldn't let you go so easily."

Dave grinned, then nodded. "She's pretty smart."

"Yes, she is. Although not so much in her own love life, I believe."

"Why's that?"

"Because I think she's fallen for Christian."

"Oh shit," he muttered. "I'll kill her."

"David, it might not be a bad thing, you know."

"How could it not be, Susan? He's a player—I thought she was too."

"She is. But I think that might be just what Christian needs, someone who can match him at his own game."

Dave looked at her for a long moment, surprised that she could be so objective about a man she loved. "Would that bother you?"

"What?"

"If she could keep him."

Susan thought about it for a moment, then shook her head. "It's not a competition. If she's the better woman for him, I love him enough to want what's best for him. I think he wants the same for me. And now I've found the man I want." She said the last staring directly into his eyes.

"Me?" he asked, grinning.

"You."

"So I owe you, huh?"

"You owe me."

"You like jewelry?" he asked, smiling as he kissed her. She laughed and kissed him back. They spent another hour kissing and cuddling.

They were both asleep when the phone rang. Dave groaned at the intrusion, then again when he glanced over and realized it was his undercover line. There was a third groan as he sat up and the headache hit him. He picked up the phone.

"Yeah?" he said, not sounding altogether happy, which he wasn't.

Susan turned on her side and put her hand on his leg. He grinned at her as he listened to the other person talk. "When?" he asked. He made a face at whatever the other person said. "Wait, is that the stuff that got botched? No, man, if that's the shit, I don't want it," he said, his eyes narrowing. "Bullshit. I want a chemist there to test it then." He listened again. "No chem, no deal, man, simple as that." There was a long pause, then he nodded, his lips curling in a sardonic *I gotcha* grin. "Yeah, okay, then when do you want to do it?" He looked highly unhappy with the time the caller named. "Jesus, you like draggin' your ass outta bed at that hour? Yeah, yeah, I'll be there.

Yeah, I can get the money. I'll see you then."

He hung up. "I gotta go back to work," he said, kissing Susan softly on the lips.

"When?"

"In the morning."

"David…" she said, sounding worried. "You just got back."

"I know. It's okay—it's a one-day kind of thing," he said, kissing her again.

She grinned. "But you'll be hungover."

"Oh yeah, pick on me now," he said, laughing as he pulled her into his arms, kissing her again. He gazed down at her. "Still love me?"

"Yes," she said, smiling.

He grinned and kissed her again. Before long they were making love. Then they slept, she on her side, curled up against his chest, he holding her. When he had to get up, he did so carefully so as not to wake her. He took his shower and got dressed. When he was ready to leave he walked over and kissed her softly on the cheek. She stirred slightly but didn't wake. He stood looking down at her for a long time. Her hair was fanned out on the pillow, with one long tendril lying over her cheek. He reached down, brushing it aside with his fingertips. She was incredibly beautiful, and he knew he'd found what he'd been looking for. As he stood there in the morning sunlight, he lifted the chain that held his cross off his neck. Undoing the clasp, he reached down and slid it carefully under Susan's neck, careful not to disturb her sleep. He fastened the clasp, then leaned down to kiss her again.

She stirred and looked up at him, not realizing what he'd just done with the necklace. "Are you leaving already?" she asked softly.

"Yeah," he said, gently touching her cheek. "Still love me?" he asked with a grin.

"Yes, David, I still love you."

"Good," he said, smiling. He kissed her again. "I'll be back later today, okay?"

She nodded. "Be careful."

"I'm always careful," he replied. He kissed her once again, and then was gone.

Susan lay where she was for a long time, just thinking about him and what had transpired the night before. Finally she stretched and rolled onto her back. That's when she felt the cold metal of the cross on her skin.

Sitting up, she picked up the cross and looked down at it. She recognized it as Dave's. She smiled to herself, thinking it was his "payment" for what he owed her. She got up and went to take a shower, then headed back over to Joe and Randy's to start her day.

Joe saw the cross first, almost dropping his coffee when she walked into the kitchen. Randy had left for school before Susan had come back out of her room that morning. Susan had decided to wear a light sweater since it was chilly, and since the cross was so long, she'd pulled it out over the top of the sweater. So there was no missing the exquisitely detailed Celtic cross. And there was no mistaking whose it was.

Joe sat down at the table, staring openmouthed at her for a long moment.

"That's Dave's," he said unnecessarily.

"I know," Susan said, smiling as she got herself some coffee. When she looked back at Joe she saw that he was staring at her. Then he nodded slowly, as if affirming something to himself.

"He gave it to you?" he asked, his voice awed.

"Yes," Susan said, her brows furrowing at his odd tone.

Joe just nodded again. He didn't comment further, leaving the kitchen and the house a few minutes later.

Susan got the children ready for school, fixed them breakfast, and did all the things she usually did. After she had dropped the children off, Susan made a decision. She needed to tell her aunt and uncle about her and Dave. She had time before her class that morning, and she was fairly sure Joe would say something to them at some point, and she'd rather it came from her.

She walked into her aunt's outer office, smiling at Cassandra. "Is she in?" Susan asked.

"Yes, she's with Lieutenant Debenshire."

Susan nodded, walking over to Midnight's door and knocking, thinking this was perfect—she could tell them both at the same time.

Midnight called for her to come in, so she opened the door. Midnight looked very surprised to see her.

"Susan…" she said, standing up and moving to hug her niece, her eyes going to the cross. When they parted, Midnight gave her a searching look.

Rick stood then to hug Susan too. He pulled up short when he saw the cross, his mouth dropping open.

"That's Dave's cross."

Susan sighed, rolling her eyes. "Why does everyone keep saying that today?"

Midnight laughed nervously, giving her husband a quelling look. She'd called him up there to tell him what Joe had called her to tell her just a few minutes before. Joe had been happy to report that he had been right about Dave and Susan and that the proof hung around Susan's neck. Midnight hadn't been sure exactly what Joe had meant, but as soon as she'd seen Susan, she knew. She hadn't had a chance to tell Rick anything before Susan had knocked though. Rick had been caught totally off guard. It was obvious in the way he moved to sit back down, as if he'd just been hit in the stomach.

"I came here to tell you that Dave and I are seeing each other," Susan said, standing there looking quite grown up at that moment.

"You can say that again," Rick muttered.

"What?" Susan asked, not hearing him clearly.

"Susan," Midnight interrupted, throwing Rick a look that said *Shut up!* "It's just kind of a shock to us, is all..." she said, trailing off as she realized she didn't know what to say either.

Susan nodded. "I understand that it might be a bit of a surprise."

"Might?" Rick echoed disbelievingly, sounding near frantic. Then he narrowed his eyes at her. "How long has this been going on?"

"Well," Susan said, starting to wring her hands, distressed at her uncle's reaction. "Since I was over to help out after his accident..." she said, her voice trailing off as Rick started to nod, looking irritated and giving Midnight a narrowed look.

"Oh, stop it!" Midnight said, giving him a dirty look.

"Uncle Rick," Susan began, seeing that this was going to cause some friction with her aunt and uncle. "Please understand that I am an adult and I know how to handle things. David is a very good man—surely you know that, having worked with him for so long…"

Rick looked disgruntled at having that pointed out, but then nodded his agreement. "I just want to know one thing," he said after a long pause.

"Yes?" Susan queried, worried.

"Do you love him?" Rick asked, his voice softer than it had been before.

Susan looked at her aunt, who was watching her expectantly, and then back to her uncle. "Yes, I love him," she said with all the conviction in her heart.

Rick nodded, standing up and walking over to her. Without a word he hugged her. When they parted he looked down at her, his eyes trailing to the cross again, then back to her eyes. "Then I'm happy for you," he said softly. Midnight hugged her again too.

Susan felt a huge sense of relief. She'd been terrified that her uncle would go crazy and threaten to kill Dave. She knew how Rick felt about her marrying someone from a good family. He'd been crazed when he'd found out about her sleeping with Christian. It had taken Joe and Midnight to contain Rick at the wedding Christian had interrupted. Now she was seeing Dave, and Dave was much older than her, not from a good family, and a police officer on top of that. But she loved him, and that was obviously enough for her uncle.

She left Midnight's office a few minutes later, not seeing the serious look that passed between her aunt and uncle as she did. Susan decided to go by Christian's office and see if Stevie was there, wanting to thank her for her advice. Stevie was in, and she glanced up at her as she walked in, her eyes going straight to the cross.

Susan held up her hand before Stevie could speak. "Yes, it's Dave's cross," she said, smiling.

Stevie nodded, looking very taken aback. "I know," she said, standing up.

Christian was working at the computer as usual, and was looking between the two of them, his expression bewildered.

"I just wanted to stop by and thank you both for the support yesterday," Susan said, reaching out to touch Christian's shoulder.

"Everything's okay?" he asked, looking doubtful.

Susan smiled. "Everything's fine."

Stevie grinned. "I'll say." She hugged Susan. "I'm glad everything worked out."

"Me too," Susan said. She leaned down and kissed Christian on the cheek. "Thank you," she whispered.

He still wore a look of total confusion, but he said, "Uh-huh."

Susan breezed out a few minutes later.

Christian glanced back at Stevie, who was standing as if rooted to the spot, staring after Susan.

"What?" he asked.

"She's wearing Dave's cross," Stevie said by way of explanation.

"So?"

"So?" Stevie echoed, looking at him like he was nuts. "So, I think that means your girl is officially off the market now." With that Stevie turned and sat back down at the desk, getting back to work.

Christian stared at Stevie's back for a long time, trying to assimilate what she'd just said. He still wasn't altogether sure what she meant, but knew that the thing between Susan and Dave was indeed serious. It was a bit of a shock.

Susan was sitting in the computer lab, working on a complicated search program for a project she was doing for her class, when her uncle walked up.

"Susan," he said when she didn't notice him.

Most everyone else in the lab had seen him. He was a very noticeable figure with his long hair, faded jeans, the shoulder holster with the nasty-looking gun inside, and his badge clipped to his belt.

Susan saw the drawn look on his face. "What?" she asked nervously, the color draining from her cheeks.

"Let's go outside," he said, extending his hand.

She took his hand and he led her toward the front of the school, where his Mustang was parked.

"Uncle Rick?" she queried as she stopped dead in her tracks, her worry overcoming her patience.

Rick stopped, glancing over his shoulder before turning and walking back to her.

"Susan, there's been an incident," he said. "We don't have all the details yet. Joe and Spider have gone over to lock down the scene, but…" He took her hands in his. "Dave's been hurt."

"What?" Susan whispered, her hands starting to shake.

Rick started walking toward the car again. He opened the door for her, and after getting in on the driver's side, he turned to her.

"He had a deal set up, but he wanted to test the stuff he was buying. The dealer chose to have the deal at the meth lab where the product is made, because he couldn't find a chemist to come with him. Anyway, something happened, and there was an explosion."

"Oh lord…" Susan said, closing her eyes.

"We don't know anything yet, Susan, okay? You're gonna have to hold it together." He reached across and touched her hand. She nodded, swallowing convulsively.

"I'm going to take you over to the department. We'll get word there, okay?" he said gently.

Susan nodded again. "What about the children?" she asked, realizing she needed to pick them up in just under an hour.

"Marie will take care of that, don't worry," Rick said, starting the Mustang with a roar and pulling away from the curb.

Ten minutes into the drive, Rick's cell phone rang. He hit the hands free. "Debenshire."

"Rick, you got her?" Midnight asked.

"Yeah, she's here," he said, glancing over at Susan.

"Susan, we're still waiting for word, okay? Joe and Spider are there now. They said they found Dave, that he was hurt but he was alive. The ambulance is taking him to the hospital now."

Rick nodded. "Mercy?"

"Yes," Midnight replied.

"Okay, we'll head there now."

"Susan?" Midnight queried.

"Yes?" Susan responded faintly.

"Just keep the faith—he'll be okay."

Susan didn't respond, only nodding.

"We'll see you there," Rick said.

"Rick, pick up," Midnight said.

Rick picked up the handset. "Yeah?"

"Spider says he looks bad."

Rick closed his eyes for a moment, then nodded. "Okay."

"Just get her there. We'll take it as it comes."

"I will. See you there."

They hung up.

Susan looked over at him. "She said he's badly hurt, didn't she?" she asked tremulously.

Rick looked at her for a long moment, then nodded. "But that doesn't necessarily mean anything. Everything looks worse on the scene. I mean, three years ago, when Midnight's car exploded and Donovan was thrown through a plate-glass window, the news reported him as critical because when they brought him into the hospital, he was covered in blood. But as it turned out, he was fine. He could be just fine, okay?"

Susan nodded, appreciating what he'd just told her. She was frightened, but she knew her uncle knew much more about this kind of thing than she did.

Rick changed freeways and headed for the hospital. When they were halfway there, his phone rang again. Again he hit the hands free. "Debenshire."

"Rick, it's Joe."

"Hey, man."

"Midnight call you?"

"Yeah, she called. How's he doing?"

"The ambulance is on the way. Spider is with him. The house is gone, man," Joe said, his tone indicating his disbelief. "But it looks like Dave got out before it blew—he dove out a window, saved a kid while he was at it."

Rick nodded. "Okay, thanks, man. We're headed to the hospital now."

Back at the department, Stevie was striding to her car, yelling to Christian, who was having a cigarette out back. He came jogging up. "What's up?"

"Dave's been hurt, let's go," she said, pulling her keys out.

Christian fell into step just behind her.

They got to her car and she got in, starting it immediately. Christian got in on the passenger side. "What happened?" he asked as she pulled out of the parking space.

Stevie shook her head. "The radio call said an explosion at a meth lab."

"Shit. What about Susan?" he said, realizing that she'd need to be told.

Stevie nodded. "Rick put in a call that he was headed over to pick her up. They're en route to the hospital now."

Christian nodded, noting the way she was gripping the wheel. He touched her shoulder. "He'll be okay, Steve."

"He better be," she said, taking a deep breath and blowing it out slowly.

At the hospital, Rick parked in front, showing the security guard his badge. He escorted Susan through the front doors and back to the emergency room. Spider met them. Unexpectedly, he hugged Susan, feeling for her. Everyone already knew about Susan having Dave's cross. Spider was Dave's best friend, so he knew better than anyone how much Susan must mean to Dave if he'd gifted it to her. Spider could see by the look on Susan's face that she was extremely upset, and he wanted to try and comfort her.

"When they brought him in they said his vital signs are good," Spider said. "He didn't get caught in the explosion, Susan. He got out in time. I'm sure he's going to be just fine, okay?"

Susan nodded numbly.

"When should we know something?" Rick asked Spider.

"The doctor went in to see him a few minutes ago, talking about X-rays and stuff, so hopefully inside an hour."

Rick nodded, squeezing Susan's shoulders.

Christian and Stevie arrived at the hospital at the same time as Joe. The two men shook hands, and Joe nodded to Stevie, giving her a small smile.

"How is he?" Christian asked as they made their way to the elevators.

"Spider says he's with the doctor now," Joe said, looking at Stevie and realizing she was very worried too. "His vital signs were good when he got here, Stevie. He'll be okay."

Stevie nodded. "Thanks."

When they got up to the floor, Christian walked over to Susan, who immediately leaned against him. His arm went around her protectively. He extended his hand to Rick, and Rick shook it, nodding.

Midnight arrived a few minutes later and got an update. She hugged Susan. The rest of the crew arrived shortly thereafter, including Donovan and Erin, Kyle and Rhiannon. Midnight glanced around, taking note of Stevie and Erin, and seeing that Kyle and Rhiannon were sitting together. The family was growing.

The doctor came out a little while later. "Dibbins?" he asked, not sure who all these people in the waiting room were here for. All of them looked up. Midnight took the lead as usual.

"He's one of my people. How is he?" she asked, reaching over to take Susan's hand.

"Mr. Dibbins is just fine," the doctor said, smiling. "He's going to have one heck of a headache for a few days, between the concussion he received and the fumes he breathed in, but otherwise he's just fine. We stitched up some cuts and made sure there was nothing major going on, but he's doing okay."

Everyone in the room breathed a sigh of relief.

"And we can see him when?" Midnight asked.

"You can go in now, if you'd like," the doctor said, gesturing to the room he'd just come from.

Susan was the first one to the door, going through it before anyone else could get there. Midnight held up her hand to the others. "Let's give them a minute, huh?"

Susan saw Dave sitting on the edge of the bed. He wasn't wearing a shirt, and there were a few cuts on his back. She walked around the bed so she could see his face. He looked up.

"Hey, babe," he said tiredly.

"David…" Susan said as she wrapped her arms around him. Dave hugged her back.

"I'm okay, honey. I'm okay," he said softly.

"You damned well better be," Rick said from the doorway.

Dave glanced back at him and saw the look on Rick's face. Midnight stood next to him, smiling. Dave nodded, understanding that they accepted his being with Susan. That was good, considering what he wanted to do.

"I see you got my present," he said, lifting the cross.

"Yes, and I caused quite a stir with it as well," Susan said, glancing back at her uncle.

"I imagine so, considering…"

"Considering what?" Susan asked, looking into his eyes.

Dave grinned. "Well, considering they all know that to me that's basically the equivalent of an engagement ring."

"To what?" Susan asked, not sure she'd heard him correctly.

Dave looked back at her for a moment, then brought his face right down to hers. "Marry me, Susan. I need you."

Susan stared at him openmouthed for a minute, not realizing that just about everyone in the room was holding their breath, including Dave. "David, are you serious?"

Dave laughed, if nothing else to relieve the tension he felt. "Yes,

Susan, I'm very serious. I need you, I love you, and I want you with me."

"Put that way…" she said, smiling at him. "My answer is yes."

Someone in the back of the room said, "Thank God." Dave was sure it was Spider.

He hugged her to him, kissing her softly. "I love you," he whispered.

"I love you too, David," Susan whispered back.

CHAPTER 3

Everyone seemed happy with the development between Dave and Susan—everyone except Christian. He took off out of the hospital as soon as he could, calling a cab to take him back to the department to pick up his car. Stevie found him four hours later at the bar in Pacific Beach that he frequented, where he knew the bartender. He was well and truly drunk by then. He'd already been in two fights, and his lip was bleeding from the second one. Stevie literally dragged him out of the building. She drove his car back to his place, figuring her Trans Am would be safer in the lot at the bar than his Viper would. Once inside his room he went for the whiskey in his cabinet.

"Oh, no," Stevie said, pulling him away.

"Just go," he said, his words slurred.

"Just shut up, Collins," she said, pushing him toward the bed. Once there, she shoved him down to a sitting position. She took off his boots, reached behind him, and pulled the gun out of the holster at the small of his back, then took it over to the cabinet he kept it in and put it away. When she walked back to him he was just sitting there, staring into space.

"Collins?"

His light blue eyes looked at her and through her. He shook his head, as if denying something to himself.

"What?" she asked, reaching out to touch him on the cheek. He jerked his head away. "Jesus!" she said, taken aback by his reaction.

He looked at her then, his eyes betraying all the pain he was feeling. Seeing it hurt her, because she knew he was hurting because he'd lost Susan. She turned away from the look in his eyes, taking small, gasping breaths. She was stunned at how much it hurt, knowing that he really did want Susan—it was actual physical pain.

Without a word she left. She didn't look back; she didn't care what happened after that. She walked out to the front of Joe's house, then kept walking. She was halfway down the winding road that led to the main street before she had the conscious thought to call a cab. By then she had no idea where she was. She kept walking until she reached a main cross street, then called for a taxi to take her back to the bar to get her car.

Once in her car she started it with a roar. The Darren Hayes CD she'd been listening to began to play; unfortunately for the CD, it happened to be on the song "Insatiable." She ejected the disk, broke it in half, and threw it out the window. She pulled out her Nickelback CD and put that in the player, cranking the song "This Is How You Remind Me." The track chronicled heartbreak and what it did to a person. It was truly how she felt at that point.

What was she to him? A good lay? Was that it? The questions kept coming into her head, and she wanted them to go away. She pushed the 5.7-liter engine to its limits, driving wherever the turns took her. The angry, searing music pumping out of the Monsoon speakers soothed her injured heart. By the time she pulled into the driveway at her sister's house, she knew exactly what she needed to do.

The following morning, she didn't go to the department. She

called and talked to Kyle, telling him she had some personal business to take care of. That day she went out and found herself an apartment. By the time Rhiannon came home that evening, Stevie had most of her stuff moved to the new place and was breaking down her bed.

"What's going on?" Rhiannon asked, standing in the doorway to the bedroom.

"I'm moving," Stevie said breathlessly. She was wrestling with a bed that weighed three times what she did.

"I've got that part," Rhiannon said as she moved to assist her sister. "Why now?"

"I just feel the need."

Rhiannon looked at her long and hard. She'd known Stevie all her life, and she knew that O'Neil fire when she saw it. "What happened? What are you running from?"

Stevie looked up at her sister sharply, but then realized that Rhiannon was simply asking—she didn't know anything. She shrugged. "Nothing, sis. I'm just feeling the need to be out on my own again. You know... be free."

Rhiannon narrowed her eyes at Stevie, knowing she was bullshitting her but not sure how to call her on it. Finally she nodded. If Stevie wanted to go, she knew there was nothing she could do to stop her. They finished the bed and Rhiannon helped her haul it out to the truck Stevie had rented. Stevie was in her own apartment by nine o'clock that night.

When she signed in to the chat room, Christian immediately instant messaged her.

Where the fuck have you been?

69

Excuse me? she typed back.

Where were you?

Are you my boss now?

Stevie, where were you?

Don't worry about it. We have work to do. I want to set these take-downs for this week.

This week?

Yeah, this week.

Which ones?

All of them. I want out of this assignment.

The cursor on the screen blinked at her for a moment, and she could almost feeling him thinking. Then came his response.

Okay, what the fuck is going on?

I'm working, Collins. I don't have time for this.

With that she closed the instant message box then put his nickname on ignore, so he could no longer message her. She made a point of talking to each guy in the room that was a target. Then she whispered them, telling them that she wanted to meet. She kept notes of each meeting time and place, setting them all up in a row, on the same day, fifteen minutes apart. When she was done she emailed Christian with a list of the take-downs and the time. Then she turned the computer off and went to bed. She didn't know that he had called Rhiannon's apartment to get ahold of her, and when he got no answer on her line, called Rhiannon. She had told him that Stevie had moved out that day and that no, she didn't have the address or Stevie's new number yet.

Christian hung up the phone with a very sick feeling in his stomach. He knew, somehow, that he'd blown it. He wasn't sure what he'd done; he only vaguely remembered the night before, and that she had gotten him home and then left. He didn't remember saying anything to her. Why had she left? He had no idea, but he intended to find out what was going on.

The following day, Stevie made an appointment with Joe and Kyle to explain about the take-downs. Kyle because he was her boss at that point, and Joe because he would be the one to come up with the backup for the bust.

Joe noted a difference in her instantly. She was closed off and cool. It reminded him of Midnight when she was mad; it was eerie how much she was like Midnight. She was business-like in the meeting, outlining the five suspects, explaining what had made her single them out. She handed Kyle the logs she'd kept and explained that Christian Collins would have the rest of them. She gave them the date of the take-downs, in two days, and the time and location. After the meeting, she thanked Kyle and Joe for their time and left Kyle's office.

When she got out to her car, Christian was there, leaning against the trunk.

"You going to tell me what's going on now?" he asked.

Stevie didn't even look at him, walking past him to the driver's side.

He walked up behind her, putting his hands on her shoulders. She spun around and brought her arm up and through, knocking away his hands effectively. She took a step back, her head coming up, a sure sign she was ready for a fight.

"Jesus Christ!" he exclaimed. "What the fuck is wrong with you?"

Her eyes were a blazing emerald fire as she looked at him. "Not a thing is wrong with me, Mr. Collins. Now get away from my car."

"Bullshit," he said, taking a step toward her and moving to her side, causing her to turn and back up, which put her up against her car.

He set his hands down on the hood on either side of her body, leaning down to her. "Tell me what's wrong, Stevie," he said, his tone still commanding.

"Back off, Collins," she said through clenched teeth.

"No, talk to me," he said, his voice as unyielding as his body.

He wasn't ready for the sharp jab she gave him to the mid-section. It knocked the wind out of him and left him coughing as she moved past him and got into her car. He straightened up as she started the engine with a roar. She didn't look at him again as she pulled out of the parking space and sped off. He leaned back against his own car, parked next to where hers had been, holding his abdomen and looking up at the sky, trying to catch his breath. He had done something wrong, that was for sure.

Two days later Stevie was set to do the busts for the chat room case. Normally, Christian wouldn't have been involved in an enforcement action, but he decided to don his badge for this one. He wanted to make sure Stevie was safe, but he wouldn't have admitted to it if someone had held a gun to his head.

The meetings and the take-downs went as planned, until the last one. The man that showed up to meet Stevie was very brawny. "Holy shit," was her whispered comment on the wire.

Joe grinned on his end, glancing over at Christian. He was fairly sure his cousin had been burned pretty bad by Ms. O'Neil; he'd heard a few things from people in the department. He'd also heard the rumor that Stevie had all but decked Christian in the parking lot when he'd backed her into a corner. She sounded more and more like Midnight all the time.

Stevie proceeded with the meeting, ensuring that the man indicated that he thought she was only sixteen. This one even said he'd like to take pictures of her if she wanted to be a star. She gave the signal for the take-down, saying "Slammin'" on the wire. But something went wrong. The guy got scared or something, because before the team could move in, he jumped up and grabbed Stevie by the arm, ready to drag her out of there.

"Go, go!" Joe yelled at the team, hearing the scuffle over the wire. Christian was right behind the backup team, as was Joe.

They got there in time to see Stevie pull back from the hold the man had on her, bringing her fist up and slamming him in the face. The man didn't go down, but he did let go of her. Once free, Stevie reached over and picked up the nearest heavy wrought-iron chair, turned it around, and jammed the legs into the man's stomach, making him double over. Stevie took the momentum and shoved him to the floor, sitting on his back and yanking his arm behind him. The raid team got there then and took over. Stevie stood up, rubbing her arm where the man had grabbed her. She stepped back as they hauled him up off the floor in cuffs.

"You bitch!" the man spat at her.

"Oh, sweetheart, I'm beyond bitch," Stevie replied, her green eyes blazing.

Joe and Christian walked up then, Christian hanging back a pace.

"You okay?" Joe asked, looking down at Stevie, quite impressed by what he'd seen.

She took a deep breath, blew it out, and then nodded. "I think I'd like the rest of the day off though, okay?" she said, feeling the need to soak her already aching muscles.

"You got it," Joe said, grinning. "You did good, O'Neil. Very good."

"Thanks," she said, smiling. For Joe Sinclair to compliment her was a huge bonus.

She walked out to her car. Christian caught up to her there.

"You really okay?" he asked, his eyes appraising her.

Stevie's face turned to stone as she turned to look at him. "I'm fine, Collins." Her eyes dropped to the badge he wore, taking on a caustic look. "You actually wear that? I thought you didn't want to be a real cop." With that she turned and got into her car. Christian stood there, staring after her as she started the Trans Am and pulled away.

He had no idea where all the venom had come from, but he had the feeling he was going to see a lot of it if he intended to keep trying to contact her.

He talked to Joe about it on the way back to the office.

"It's like she hates me now," Christian said, shaking his head.

Joe looked over at him, assessing what his cousin had told him. Christian had explained how he and Stevie had been spending a lot of time together. The discussion included the fact that great sex was involved. Christian had also mentioned that he liked that Stevie

74

wasn't clingy, expecting some kind of commitment.

"Well," Joe said, turning back to his driving, "you always said you wanted to know what it would be like to be with Midnight…"

"Yeah," Christian said, staring at his cousin. "But what's Stevie got to do with that?"

Joe grinned. "You're seeing the same kind of fire Rick lives with every day."

Christian looked back at Joe for a long moment, his brows furrowed. He nodded. "I've just developed a new respect for Rick Debenshire."

Joe laughed. "Women like that are rare, but they come at a pretty high price."

"How high?" Christian asked, near exasperation.

"Your heart, your soul, and a whole hell of a lot of your patience," Joe said wisely.

Christian nodded again, looking out the window for a while. He turned back to Joe. "So where did you say you met Randy?"

Joe laughed and shook his head. He knew Christian might be talking like he didn't want someone like Stevie because she was a lot of work, but he suspected Christian was already caught. He'd never openly agonized over a woman before, not even Susan. Midnight had had that effect on Rick too, and everyone knew what a good match they were.

***

Erin moving in with Donovan actually went smoother than either of them had expected. Bobby, hungry for a strong male role model, liked Donovan right away. Tyler had started calling Erin on a daily basis, frequently to threaten her, telling her he was going to beat the shit out of her for running off on him. She became more and more afraid. Donovan assured her that Tyler wouldn't get near her at all. Finally he went to Erin's supervisor and told her Erin needed to have her office number changed. That happened immediately, largely because the chief herself called down to reiterate the necessity, but it was only a temporary fix. It took Tyler three days to wheedle Erin's new number out of some weak-minded secretary.

Joe stepped in next, putting out a department-wide bulletin stating that a staff member was being threatened, and that the man doing it was considered dangerous. Tyler's picture was printed on the bulletin with the description Erin gave Joe. It had been Donovan who stepped the matter up, going to Joe, Midnight, and Kyle about the problem. Midnight had followed up the bulletin with a reiteration of the departmental policy of confidentiality. She explained that it was in effect for the safety of all the employees in the department, not just sworn peace officers. She further warned that anyone caught breaking this confidentiality would find themselves up on charges and without a place of employment in record time.

***

Dave and Susan were spending his recuperation time relaxing. She raised an eyebrow at him when he poured himself a Jack and Coke. He grinned unrepentantly and said, "I'm recuperating."

"I see," she said, smiling.

He sat back down on the couch next to her, stretching his long legs out in front of him.

"So what were you doing that other night?" she asked.

"Wallowing," he replied with a grin.

"I see," she said, sounding very English. "So one drink is recuperating, a bottle is wallowing."

"Two bottles."

"Two?" Susan repeated, aghast.

Dave shrugged. "The one you saw was the second one."

"David!" she exclaimed, laughing in spite of herself.

He definitely wasn't mysterious about his way of doing things. She was finding that now that they had committed to getting married, he was even more relaxed than he had been before. She had also found that she liked her husband-to-be even more than she'd even realized before. He had an easy way about him that made her feel very comfortable being totally herself with him. Case in point, the drinking. She would never have pointed out her concern about Christian having a drink, knowing it would probably cause him to tell her to back off. Dave took her concern—seemed to enjoy it, in fact—but assured her that he wasn't overdoing it. There was no defensiveness in him; he was who he was, and he allowed her to be herself too. She loved him all the more for it.

"So," he said, leaning his head back on the couch, rolling it to the side so he could look at her. "When do you want to get married?"

Susan smiled. She also liked that he was more than ready to settle down with her. He'd already told her he wanted her to move in with him as soon as possible. Even so, she was already staying with him full time, she just hadn't moved any of her things over.

"Whenever you want to," she said.

Dave looked thoughtful. "How long do these things take to plan?"

"Well, my last wedding…" Susan made a face, making Dave chuckle. "Had taken six months, and we were rushing things."

He gave her a stunned look. "Six months?"

"Yes," she replied, smiling at his expression.

He shook his head. "I don't want to marry you in front of Congress, I just want to marry you."

Susan smiled again. She loved that he was so set on making her his wife. She was reveling in the feeling of being wanted, needed, and loved.

"Well, I suppose we can simplify things a bit," she said, moving to lean against the back of the couch, turned to the side to face him, one leg tucked under her. "We need to decide where to have the wedding first."

Dave nodded, then gave her a worried look. "You're Catholic, aren't you?"

"Yes," Susan said cautiously. "Aren't you?"

"Why would you think that?"

Susan picked up the cross she still wore around her neck. "Celtic cross, David—usually indicates Irish Catholic."

Dave grinned. "Yeah, and remember what I bought that cross with, honey."

"Oh…" she said, trailing off as she realized she'd totally neglected to consider that. "So, what religion are you?"

"I'm not," he replied simply.

"Not what? Religious?" she asked, surprised for some reason.

Dave chuckled. "See, that's usually something you discuss on the fifth or sixth date."

Susan laughed. "So true." She reached out to touch his cheek, liking the way his eyes sparkled when he looked at her. "Then we won't have it in any church."

"Will your family approve of that?" he asked, concerned, aware that she was already going to have to deal with a lot, since she was marrying way below her class and marrying a man a lot older than her.

"David, I don't care if they approve or not. I love you and will marry you wherever I have to in order to be yours."

The sincerity in her statement had him feeling so happy he couldn't begin to show her. Instead he leaned forward and kissed her softly, then set his drink on the table in front of the couch and pulled her close to kiss her more deeply. They ended up lying on the couch, he against the back, on his side, she lying in his arms, looking up at him.

"What about the beach?" she asked.

"The beach?"

"Yes," she said, touching his arm, tracing the letters on his tattoo that said *IB Bad Boys*. "The beach is so much a part of you, and it's where we had our first kiss."

"And our second," he said, grinning. Then he nodded. "Sounds good, but how do you go about doing that?"

"Leave that to me, I will handle everything," Susan assured him.

"Okay, but," he said, putting his finger to her lips, "I'm paying for everything."

"David…"

"Susan, this is our wedding, our thing, no one else's. I don't want anyone paying for it but us, okay?"

Susan looked like she wanted to protest further, but then she nodded. "Then I want to pay for half."

"No."

"David," she said sternly.

"Susan," he countered equally so, though his grin spoiled the effect. "Look, I'm not some kid—I can pay for my own wedding, okay?"

"It's my wedding too."

He narrowed his eyes at her. "I'm paying for it."

She looked back at him for a long moment, seeing that she wasn't going to get very far in this discussion. Finally she sighed and nodded. "But I'm paying for the honeymoon."

Dave laughed and shook his head, seeing that she was determined. "Fine, but I'll plan it."

Susan gave him a suspicious look then, but he leaned down to kiss her again, and any suspicion she had left her head. He loved her, he wanted to take care of her—she loved that.

They spent the next few hours talking about the wedding. After a while it was apparent he was getting tired, so she led him to the bedroom and gave him medicine for his headache, which was indeed a constant at that point. She lay next to him, stroking his hair until he fell asleep. Lying there in his room, she thought about all that had happened in such a short time. In a few short weeks, in fact. Suddenly her life was about to change, and it had come from such an unexpected direction.

She knew her mother was in for a shock when she arrived in a week's time. When she'd called her mother, Deborah Endicott, she'd simply stated that she was in love and was getting married. Deborah had asked a number of questions, but Susan had said that none of that mattered. Deborah had insisted on coming to America to meet this man that her daughter planned to marry; Susan had agreed reluctantly, not sure how her mother would react to Dave. She was afraid she would come and cause a big scene about Susan marrying a man almost old enough to be her father, and a police officer from limited means on top of that. None of that mattered to Susan, but she knew it mattered to her family.

Deborah had divorced her husband of many years the year before, because she'd finally given up the facade of being happily married to a man that was more interested in making money than being in love. It hadn't left Deborah penniless; besides the money she'd received in the divorce, Deborah's family was worth a fair amount themselves, having come from a long line of wealthy people. The Debenshires weren't multi-millionaires, but there was no lack of wealth in their midst. The children—Rick, Deborah, and their two sisters—had been left trust funds by their grandmother that, under the management of their father, Robert, had become expansive portfolios worth close to a million each.

The fact that Deborah had divorced to find love didn't mean she wanted her daughter to find love with someone the family didn't find suitable. That was going to be the rub. Susan knew that her uncle Rick approved of the match superficially, but would he continue to approve in the face of strong disapproval from the rest of the family? Susan didn't know, and she was afraid of Dave being crucified in the process. She loved him enough to want to protect him from the aspersions her family could cast about him.

"So tell me about this man my daughter is marrying," Deborah Endicott said to her brother without preamble.

"It's nice to see you too, Deborah," Rick said, grinning as he leaned forward to kiss her on the cheek and take her valise.

"Oh, Richard, I'm sorry." Deborah shook her head and hugged her brother. "I just never know what to expect with Susan these days," she explained as they walked toward the baggage claim. "One minute she's in love with Christian Collins, the next she's marrying some other man."

Rick rubbed the bridge of his nose, looking contrite. "Well, it did happen rather suddenly."

Deborah looked at her brother, noting that he was anxious about something. The fact was, Rick knew Deborah had expected him to keep an eye on Susan for her, since she was so far from home. And twice Rick had failed at that job. First with Susan getting involved with Christian Collins, and again now with Dave. He hadn't known about either of them until it had been too late to suggest a different course of action for Susan or even warn Deborah.

"Well, who is this man?" Deborah asked as they waited for her bags.

Rick gave her an odd look as he reached over to grab one of her suitcases. "You've met him, Deborah. A few times, in fact."

"I have?" Deborah replied, mystified.

Rick straightened up, searching his sister's eyes. "He's worked with Midnight and me for a long time."

"He has?"

Rick shook his head, his grin wry. "Susan didn't tell you much, did she?"

"No, she only told me she was in love and getting married." Deborah's tone indicated her opinion of such an appalling lack of information.

Rick chuckled, looking heavenward. "Well, Dave's been with Midnight since the original FORS unit."

"The original..." Deborah began, her eyes widening. "My lord, that's years!"

Rick nodded. "Fourteen years."

"Fourteen?" she asked, her expression becoming more concerned. "Don't you have to be a certain age to be a police officer?"

"Uh, yeah, twenty-one."

Deborah gave her brother a stunned look. "So this man has to be at least thirty-five?"

"He's thirty-nine."

"Oh my lord!" Deborah exclaimed, causing people to turn and look at her.

Rick grinned at his sister's reaction and nodded in the direction of his car parked out front. When she reached it, Deborah looked it over. The Mustang was painted British Racing Green, and screamed speed and high-performance power from every cubic inch.

"Richard, you're going to kill yourself with your sports cars one day," was her only comment.

Rick grinned, remembering Midnight's comment about two twenty-year-olds and change.

Once in the car, Deborah turned to him. "So apart from the fact that he's almost old enough to be her father…" she began, making Rick grimace at the definition she had already attached to Dave— Midnight was going to kill him for that. "Tell me about this man. What is he like?"

"He's a good man, Deb," Rick assured her. "And he loves Susan."

"And you know this how?"

"Well…" Rick began, not sure if he should try to explain about the cross. "Dave's been a player for years. He's known in the department for having at least three girlfriends at a time."

"Richard, you're not making me feel any better," Deborah said sourly.

Rick gave her an impatient look. "Let me finish. Anyway, he's got this cross that he wears—it's something he's had forever. It's a symbol to him of the life he left behind, and it's also the key to his independence. He never takes this cross off, not even when he got shot and was in the hospital—he refused to let them take it." He gave her a pointed look then. "He gave that cross to your daughter."

"So what does that prove?"

"Deb, Dave's had hundreds of girlfriends. He's never relinquished that cross or his independence. He's done both for Susan."

Deborah looked back at him for a long moment, not sure if she was impressed by the action or not, but she nodded.

Rick took Deborah to the office, having discussed it with Midnight that morning. Midnight had told him that she wanted some time with Deborah before Deborah went to see Susan. Susan had talked to Midnight about her concerns over how her mother would react to Dave. Midnight was determined to try and help if she could. Dave was one of her best friends, and she considered him the best of the best in terms of loyalty and reliability. He'd always been there when the chips were down, and that went a long way with Midnight. She also sincerely liked him as a friend; he was very different from the other men in her life, in that he was easygoing and not so intense all the time. Dave had a way about him that made everyone around him comfortable; that was part of what made him the best narc she had.

Rick knocked on Midnight's door and walked in. Midnight was on the phone, but hung up a few moments later. She stood up and hugged Deborah; they'd become fairly close over the years. Midnight liked all of Rick's sisters, except Katherine, the oldest. Katherine and Midnight had started out on a bad foot and had never quite gotten past that. Rick told Midnight he'd see her later, leaning over to kiss his wife on the lips. Midnight looked up at him for a moment, her eyes narrowing, realizing he'd done something wrong already. He just grinned and walked out.

"So how are you?" Midnight asked Deborah as she gestured for her to sit on the couch. Midnight joined her there.

"I'm just fine," Deborah said. "Just trying to keep up with my daughters."

"How's the single life going?" Midnight asked, aware that Deborah had cited a desire for a relationship like hers and Rick's as one of the determining factors in her split with Wilson.

"It's been interesting," Deborah admitted, having just come from a weekend in Paris with a very handsome Italian count. It had been a fling, but it had been fun indeed.

Even at forty-four, Deborah was a very beautiful woman. There wasn't a line on her face; her skin was perfect. Her sapphire blue eyes, exactly like Rick's and Susan's, shone with health and happiness. Midnight was glad to see it.

"So, Midnight," Deborah began. "What is your take on this man Susan is seeing?"

Midnight sat back on the couch, giving her sister-in-law a long look. "Honestly, Deborah, I can't say one negative thing about Dave. He's a helluva guy."

Deborah nodded. "My brother tells me he's thirty-nine years old."

Midnight narrowed her eyes. "Oh, he did, did he?" she said, her tone turning slightly icy at the thought that her husband had in any way detracted from Dave being accepted by Deborah. "Did he bother to mention that Dave is the best narcotics officer I have, and one of the best and most loyal friends Rick and I have?"

"Midnight," Deborah said, holding up her hands, worried that she'd lit a fuse on her sister-in-law's temper and that her brother was about to be the target. "Rick told me that he thinks Dave is a good guy, and that he loves Susan. He wasn't trying to denigrate him in the least when he told me his age. I'm just worried that my daughter is searching for a father figure in all this."

Midnight shook her head. "No, I don't think that at all. Dave may be thirty-nine, but he is by no means an old man, no more than Rick is at thirty-seven."

Deborah smiled; that much was very true. Her brother never seemed to age at all, always full of energy and life. Deborah attributed that to his marriage to Midnight. She kept him on his toes constantly.

"Alright, that I can understand," Deborah said, nodding. "But what do they have in common?"

"Not a whole lot. But Deborah, having things in common doesn't always ensure a good marriage. You and Wilson had a number of things in common—friends, social standing, all that—did it make you happy?"

"No, it didn't. Will he be good for her?" Deborah asked, her main concern coming to bear.

"I think they'll be good for each other. And I think that's more important."

"How so?" Deborah asked, interested in Midnight's insight. Midnight saw things very differently than she did, and it was always enlightening to hear her views.

"Well, it's never a good thing for a relationship to be one-way. If he was only good for her, eventually he'd need to find something or someone else that was good for him, right?"

"I see your point," Deborah said, having not looked at it that way.

"In this case, though, I think she will be as good for him as he is for her."

"How?" Deborah asked, interested now. Curious how Midnight

would see this situation.

"The work that Dave does is very demanding. He is required to become someone that he doesn't like being in order to do the job he does. When he's undercover he has to become this persona, taking him back to something he left behind when he was much younger, because he knew it was wrong. Since the people he deals with are very dangerous and also very volatile, he has to be on his guard constantly while he's undercover. It means he doesn't sleep for days at a time, and he isn't able to communicate with regular people, or even go home to his own bed. He never gets normal meals. He has to be stuck in that mire for days, even weeks at a time. When he gets home, he needs to deprogram his mind. He needs someone who loves him and who can take care of him. He needs her. And I sincerely think that Susan needs to be needed—that's why she does what she does for a living. She enjoys nurturing someone, taking care of them. The way that they got to know each other was while she was taking care of him after an accident. I asked her to go over and make sure he didn't starve to death, because he was laid up with his back out. Susan thrives on taking care of people. And she loves him."

Deborah listened to Midnight's discourse and took comfort in the fact that her sister-in-law so obviously approved of Susan's choice for a husband. It hadn't been so with the young man, Warren, that Susan had intended to marry. Midnight had been totally against the marriage, but was willing to support Susan's decision—not to the point, however, that she didn't have anything negative to say about Warren. She'd even advised Susan to go out and test the waters sexually before she married him.

"You said he's gone undercover for weeks at a time?" Deborah asked, that one point sticking in her mind.

"He's been gone a month before," Midnight said, being honest. "But keep in mind he's never had anything to come home to but an empty house."

Deborah nodded, then sighed. "I guess I'll have to give him a chance, at least."

"Uh…" Midnight said, giving Deborah an *I have news for you* look.

"What?"

"I've talked to Susan, and she's not looking for your approval on this. She plans to marry Dave come hell or high water."

Deborah looked shocked; her daughter had always sought her approval before.

"I told you, Deb—she loves him."

"I guess so," Deborah said, shaking her head slowly.

***

Rick's phone rang in his office.

"Debenshire," he said, picking it up as he read a report.

"Is Ms. Endicott with you?" Dave asked.

"Dave? No, she's up with Midnight. Why?"

"Because I'm here to take her back to the house."

"Are you nuts?"

Dave grinned. "Sometimes."

"Dave, man, I don't think this a good idea. Is Susan with you, at least?"

"Nope," Dave answered calmly.

Rick shook his head, rolling his eyes. He was sure Dibbins had inhaled too much ether at the explosion the week before. "We need to get your head checked, man, I'm tellin' ya."

Dave chuckled. "Just let your wife know I'm headed upstairs," he said good-naturedly.

True to his word, he was knocking on Midnight's door five minutes later. Midnight called him to come in. She and Deborah stood from the couch. Dave remembered Deborah from Susan's first attempt at a wedding. He'd forgotten how much Susan looked like her mother. Deborah Endicott was much more sophisticated than Susan was at this point, but their hair and eye color were exact as well as their finely boned faces.

Dave met Deborah's eyes directly, without even a hint of intimidation. He extended his hand. "I'm Dave Dibbins. I believe we've met."

Deborah nodded and graciously took his hand. "Yes, I'm sure we have. You do look familiar now that I see you."

"Shall we go?"

Deborah nodded, taken aback by Dave's direct but polite manner.

"Rick will bring your suitcases by later," Midnight said.

"Thank you," Deborah said, hugging her sister-in-law again.

Dave and Deborah left the office. Dave held the door for her and gestured for her to precede him. It was apparent that this was not an unfamiliar action for him, since he was so comfortable in his manner.

On the way down in the elevator, she looked at him; he leaned comfortably against the wall, looking straight ahead. She could see his mind working, and she wasn't altogether sure it had anything to do with her. She tried to assimilate everything she'd been told about him that morning. He was definitely a good-looking man, with his sandy-brown hair cut short, but longer on the top. He was tall, around six feet, with a lean build. He was also very tanned, and his bright, sky blue eyes stood out in a handsome face. Dave reminded Deborah of the calendars of California you saw all over depicting surfers with tanned chests, killer smiles, and shades on their faces.

Dave led her over to the Charger, opening the door for her. She got in, looking around. She found his car an interesting choice. She could tell by the look of it that it was a classic. She didn't know enough about vehicles to know what it was, but with its long body and classic style, it seemed to fit Dave's appearance quite well. When he climbed in on the driver's side, she looked over at him. He did indeed fit his car, like a classic with spirit. She was surprised when the engine started with a deep, throaty rumble. The phrase "power under a tight rein" came to mind, and she wondered if that matched its owner as well. Classic rock played on the radio. Deborah recognized Foreigner from her brother's old favorites. The song was "Dirty White Boy"—she found it amusing; the words seemed to fit the situation perfectly. Had he planned it that way? The lyrics spoke of loving the wrong person and ruining one's reputation with him, and said that he was simply a "dirty white boy."

They were both quiet for a long time, each not sure what exactly to say. Deborah broke the silence first.

"Did my daughter send you?"

Dave turned down the radio, grinning. "Actually, she begged me not to come."

"And why is that?" Deborah asked, finding herself grinning too. His smile was contagious.

He shrugged, looking thoughtful. "She seems to think I need protection from you," he said conversationally.

"Why would she think that?" Deborah asked, knowing exactly why her daughter thought that.

Dave looked over at her, his blue eyes saying, *You know why she thinks that.* Deborah was taken aback. He was indeed direct, without being rude.

"Let me lay my cards on the table here, Ms. Endicott," Dave said, putting his hand on the dashboard in front of him. "I'm not looking for, nor do I need, your approval. I love Susan, and I have every intention of marrying her, regardless of what anyone says." He looked over at her, his face serious but with not a hint of malice. "Now, obviously it would make things easier on everyone if you and I got along, but it's not a requirement. I realize Susan is marrying someone no one would have chosen for her—hell, not even I would have chosen me for her—but she chose me and I love her for that. I will not have her put through an inquisition to determine my fitness for her as a husband. That's for her to decide, and she's made the decision."

At the end of his speech, he studied her expression. He could read surprise on her face. It hadn't been his intention to intimidate her in the least; he merely wanted her to understand that this was not some kind of appraisal. He didn't care what anyone thought. He loved Susan and she loved him—that was all that mattered. He also knew that Susan was turning herself inside out worrying about what her family would say to him to hurt him. She didn't realize that nothing anyone could say would be worse than he'd ever heard before. What mattered to him was what she said and thought, no one else.

"Well," Deborah said, smiling again in spite of herself, "thank you for your candor." She sounded like she honestly meant it. "I understand that you are quite accomplished in your profession—apparently it pays to hone your negotiating skills to the point of being quite direct about your motivations."

Dave laughed. "You could say that."

"I will say that my brother and sister-in-law think very highly of you, and since I very much respect their opinion, I was ready to give you a chance. Now I have to say that I'm quite impressed with the way you handle things. Are you this decisive with my daughter?"

"For the most part," he replied, grinning. "I have to admit, though, that she does tend to derail me every now and then."

"For example?"

"Well…" Dave leaned back comfortably in his seat, driving with his arm on the window, his hand on the wheel, the other on the gear shift. "For example, I had decided, probably for all the same reasons you probably thought I was unsuitable, that her and I shouldn't see each other anymore."

"And what were those reasons?" Deborah asked, curious how he saw himself.

"Age, social standing, backgrounds, and most of all, the fact that I couldn't get her out of my head long enough to get any work done." He said the last with a grin.

Deborah laughed. "So what happened?"

"Well, I made my speech about us not seeing each other anymore. I told her I couldn't explain it, but that we just couldn't see each other. She accepted it and left. I got drunk. She showed back up that night and basically told me she wanted an explanation. I attempted, in my inebriated condition, to explain, and she proceeded to tell me that she loved me." He pursed his lips, looking over at her. "That pretty much shut me up."

"Why?" Deborah asked, intrigued that her daughter had taken that kind of initiative. Susan hadn't even taken the initiative when she was in love with Christian but marrying Warren. It had taken Christian's interruption at the wedding and his demand that she come with him to change her mind.

"Well, it shut me up because I already knew I was in love with her—I just never believed she could feel the same way," he said, his tone both humble and wistful at the same time.

Deborah smiled. She was finding that the more he talked, the more she liked him.

"You love my daughter," she said simply.

"Ms. Endicott," Dave said, still looking quite blissful, "your daughter is..." He shook his head, as if not able to come up with a good description. "She's everything."

If Dave Dibbins had said nothing else, that alone would have won Deborah over thoroughly. It was exactly what she wanted for her daughter: a man that found nothing lacking in her. Dave was indeed the man for Susan. Midnight had been right.

When they arrived at the house, Susan came out to meet them, looking so worried it was almost painful to see. Deborah walked over to her daughter, smiling and hugging her close.

"He's wonderful, Susan," she whispered.

Susan was sure she couldn't be happier than she was at that moment. She looked over at Dave as he stood leaning against his car, smiling at them. She walked over to him, putting her arms around him and hugging him tight. "Thank you," she said, looking up into his eyes.

"For what?" he asked, his eyes searching hers.

"For whatever you said to my mother, for insisting on picking her up, for being you." She said the last standing on her tiptoes to kiss him softly on the lips. He hugged her close, enjoying the feeling of being so loved.

Deborah watched them with a full heart. Her daughter had found her true love. What more could a mother want?

Since moving into Donovan's house, Erin had found herself in his bed every night. Sex wasn't always involved, since Bobby slept just down the hall from his room, but she often went in to talk to him after Bobby had gone to sleep. Donovan always welcomed her presence. They'd often watch TV together; other times they'd talk about his latest case. He'd finished up his big case and was working on a few new ones, starting with the legwork of the preliminary information gathering.

One night, they were both asleep when the phone rang. Donovan rolled over, picking up the phone and looking at the clock at the same time. It was 1:30 a.m.

"Curtis," he said into the receiver.

"Donovan Curtis?" the caller asked.

"Yeah, this is Donovan Curtis. Who's this?" Donovan asked, moving to sit up. Erin turned over, looking up at him.

"This is Investigator Frank Dominguez of the Department of Alcoholic Beverage Control. Do you happen to have a forwarding number for Anthony and Maricella Franco?"

"Forwarding number?" Donovan asked. "No... I know they're on vacation in Mexico," he said. "What's this about?"

"You were listed as a contact on Investigator Jeanie Franco's emergency notification card, Mr. Curtis."

"What's happened to Jeanie?" Donovan asked, real concern creeping into his voice. Erin sat up.

"Well, she's been hurt. She was on a case and her suspect attacked her."

"Shit," Donovan said, closing his eyes. He knew it couldn't be minor if they were trying to get ahold of her parents. "Is she okay?"

"Well, she's pretty bruised up, with a concussion and some cracked ribs, and understandably distraught," Dominguez said. "She wanted her family contacted, since they're running a newspaper story on the incident."

"Did you get the guy that did it?" Donovan asked, anger coursing through him.

"Yes, we have him in custody."

"Good. So where is she?"

"She's still with the doctor."

"How long will she be in the hospital?"

"They're wanting to keep her overnight for observation."

"Okay. What hospital?"

"San Francisco General."

"I'll be there, thanks," Donovan said, and hung up.

Frank Dominguez stared at the receiver still buzzing with a dial tone. "Be there?" he said to no one. Who was this guy? Frank didn't like the idea of this man coming here. He had a good line on getting to Jeanie and he didn't want some would-be cowboy to come charging in to screw that up. Frank wondered belatedly if Donovan might be the ex she had talked about a few times.

"Shit," he said to himself, and went in to see Jeanie.

Four hours later Donovan stepped off a plane at San Francisco Oakland International Airport. He took a cab to the hospital and went inside. He found out which floor Jeanie was on and went directly up. When he asked for her room at the front desk, a man turned to him.

"You must be Donovan Curtis," he said, extending his hand, his look appraising. "Frank Dominguez."

Donovan nodded slowly, taking the other man's hand. He noted the predatory assessment and could tell this man was sizing him up. *Why?* he wondered.

"How's she doing?" Donovan asked.

"She's doing fine, Mr. Curtis, like I told you on the phone."

"It's sergeant," Donovan found it necessary to put in. "And yeah, thanks for the call. What room is she in?"

Frank Dominguez noted the correction and found himself irritated that someone this young-looking was a sergeant. Frank hadn't ever made sergeant in his ten years with San Francisco PD; that was why at thirty-five he'd joined Alcoholic Beverage Control, so he could say he was an investigator. With nothing else he could do, Frank pointed toward the door to Jeanie's room, and followed a few steps behind Donovan as he walked over.

Donovan knocked softly as he opened the door. Jeanie was sitting up with her legs dangling over the side of the bed. She was wearing street clothes that were ripped and dirty. She had her back to him, and didn't even glance back to see who it was.

"I can't stay here," she said without preamble.

Donovan walked around the side of the bed just then, and Jeanie's breath caught in her throat. He was the last person she'd expected to see. Frank stood watching at the door. Neither of them noticed.

"Donovan?" Jeanie said, her face reflecting her astonishment.

"Hey, Jay," he said, taking in the bruises on her face and the cut on her cheek, his eyes reflecting his pain at seeing them.

Jeanie took a deep breath, trying hard to control the desire to leap into his arms. She lost that control when he stepped forward, taking her into a gentle hug. The tears flowed then.

"Donovan... Donovan..." she chanted, holding on to him for dear life.

"It's okay, Jay, it's okay," he said, stroking her hair carefully, not wanting to hurt her any more than she already had been.

"Please take me out of here," she said against his shirt.

"Are you sure?" he asked, worried that she was more injured than she looked.

"The doctor says I'm fine—he just wants to keep me just in case.

I don't want to stay here, Donovan, please," she said, lifting her head and looking into his eyes.

"Okay, babe, okay," he said, and lifted her up in his arms. She clung to his neck, resting her head against his shoulder.

Frank wanted to stop the guy from taking her, but he'd heard her himself; she had begged this Donovan to take her away. What could he do? He'd call her tomorrow morning or maybe go over to her place to see how she was.

Donovan managed to get her to her apartment, but no sooner had he opened the door and carried her in than she told him she wanted to go home.

"You are home, Jay," he said, thinking the meds were messing with her head. Her apartment was a studio, so it was fairly easy for him to locate the bed in the corner behind a Japanese bathing screen. He set her down carefully.

"No, Donovan, I mean I want to go home to San Diego," she said, her voice a soft plea. "I hate it here—I just want to go home."

"Babe, there's no one *at* home," he said sympathetically. "Your parents are out of town, and God only knows where your brothers are."

"I don't care," Jeanie said, sounding increasingly panicked. "I have a key to my parents' house. I need to get out of here. Please, Donovan?"

"Okay," he said placatingly. "You lie down, and I'll make some calls."

She nodded and lay down obediently. Donovan pulled out his cell phone and started calling. A little while later he sat down on the bed next to her.

"I'm sorry, babe. The soonest I can get us a flight back out is tomorrow night. Everything's booked right now."

Jeanie looked devastated, but she nodded miserably.

"We could drive," Donovan said, trying to make her feel better.

"I can't ask you to do that…" Jeanie said, but he caught the ray of hope in her eyes.

He shrugged. "It's only nine hours away. I figured I'd be here a couple of days anyway."

"Are you sure?" she asked, looking honestly concerned.

"Yeah, no problem."

Donovan rented a car, a nice spacious Bonneville so she'd have room to relax on the drive. He called Spider to tell him what was going on and request a few days off. Then he called Erin to let her know what he was doing. She was, as always, supportive, telling him to drive carefully. Donovan also called Joe, and asked him to keep an eye on Erin for him while he was gone. Joe told him he'd have patrol check on her every hour in the evening and at night.

"Thanks, man," Donovan said, ever grateful for his family.

Jeanie and he were headed out of town three hours later. As he got on the freeway, she reached over and touched his arm. "Thank you," she said softly. "For coming, for doing this… for everything." She looked like she was ready to cry. She turned away then, looking out the window, and was silent for a long time.

The traffic getting out of San Francisco was extremely heavy. It took four hours alone to get out of the bay area. During that time Donovan skimmed around on radio stations. They didn't really talk much. Jeanie had brought her CDs, so they pulled out a few and put them in the player. After the second disk Donovan saw that she had the new Darren Hayes CD; he had it too, and liked it, so he put it on. He sang along with "Strange Relationship," grinning to himself when he remembered the Jeanie exorcism conversation with Erin.

Jeanie watched him singing and thought he might be talking about her and him. She didn't comment. When the third track came on she noted that he knew every word, and it sounded far too close to home. The song was about betrayal and the other person doing whatever they chose, while others around them were "left to bleed." She knew Donovan meant her this time.

Up until that point she'd liked the song, but seeing Donovan sing it made her realize again how screwed up her priorities had gotten. The line "You do whatever you please, everybody else is left to bleed" was true enough. She'd left him to go after a career. He'd warned her that she was trying to go too far too fast, and he'd been right. He'd told her she needed street time to learn how to handle situations; he'd been right. She'd insulted him by saying he was jealous. God, she was so stupid. And even more mortifying, when she needed him, here he was. No anger, no guilt, no questions, he was just there.

She'd realized pretty early on that she had made a mistake. By the time she'd reached the academy in Long Beach she'd been ready to turn around and run back to Donovan. But she'd stayed; she'd committed to taking this job, and she was going to at least see the academy through. She'd made it, but not without feeling every day like she didn't belong there. She'd found out quickly that she was there because she was female, nice-looking, and Hispanic. It had nothing to do with any abilities they thought she had. She found herself in a class with men that either wanted to lay her or hated her because she was young and already getting an investigator position. Many of them had been street cops for years in departments that didn't promote them. She'd been a street cop out of the academy a little over six months. They treated her like a fluff without a brain.

When she'd gone home after the academy she'd wanted to talk to someone about how she was feeling, but her brothers had told her to deal with it, that women were always treated differently in law enforcement. She'd even gone to see Erin, in the hopes that she would lend a sympathetic ear, but that had been when she'd run into her with Donovan. She had decided she needed to stay away from San Diego for a while, which was why she had gone ahead and gone to the San Francisco assignment.

Once again, the guy she was partnered with, Frank Dominguez, wanted to screw her, and at the same time he hated her for having the chance he'd never gotten until he was thirty-five. She'd staved him off, but he was always calling her and trying to get her to go out with him. She couldn't stand it. It also showed her, graphically, that she'd had the best she could have in San Diego, and she'd been on the right track but had gotten stupid and impatient, and now she'd lost everything. She knew Donovan had called Erin at his own house because she'd seen it on the caller ID screen when she'd walked by him. So he was living with Erin now. She'd lost him. She wanted to scream and shout, and beg him to take her back, but she knew she'd blown it one too many times. Her past history with him was coming back to haunt her.

She couldn't escape her mistakes with Donovan. She'd ruined it; it had been her fault entirely. She knew that, and knew she had to learn to accept it. So she hoped that with this time with him, she'd at least be able to make friends with him again. She needed to talk to someone, and Donovan had been her very best friend for over a year. He hadn't portrayed any lingering anger over the breakup, and she hoped that meant that in moving on, he'd at least gotten over the anger. His scathing words that day at the department had hurt, but she knew she'd deserved what he had said and much more. But as usual, Donovan was too much of a gentleman to actually say what he felt.

That was why she knew that the fact that he knew every word of the song "Heart Attack" meant that he felt that way about her. Her hope plunged a bit then.

They were two hours out of the bay area when Donovan pulled over at a rest stop. Jeanie got out and went into the bathroom. When she came out she didn't see Donovan at first. She walked around the other side of the small building the bathrooms were housed in and saw him standing with his back to the wall, his arm up on the bricks beside him, his head down.

"Donovan?" she said.

His head came up, and she could see he was in pain. It hit her then.

"Oh, Donovan, your back..." she said, feeling like the worst human being in the world. She'd managed to totally forget the problems he'd had with his back ever since the incident three years before when the car bomb had thrown him twenty feet and through a plate-glass window. There had been a lot of muscle damage that had healed but had made it so he couldn't sit for long periods of time without his muscles knotting severely, causing him almost disabling pain. There had been many times when she would spend hours trying to work out the knots in his back. He'd had to take Flexeril and Vicodin just to be able to sleep.

She walked over, standing in front of him. "Tell me what I can do," she said, willing to do anything at that point.

He shook his head. "I'm okay," he said, but the sound of his voice belied the pain he was in.

"No, you're not. Jesus, Donovan, I'm so sorry. I never even thought about how long it would take to drive, and that you'd have to sit the whole time. God, I'm sorry."

"Jay, it's okay," he said, moving around to stretch the muscles in his back. He had been fighting off nausea when she'd come around the corner.

"Okay, I'm going to drive. I want you to lie down in the back seat."

"Jay…"

"I don't want to hear it. You're in pain because of me. The least I can do is take over the driving." Then she made a decision. "Okay, we're going to go to a hotel, too. You need to take a hot shower or you're going to be worse."

She looked for the nearest decent-sized town and found them a hotel. Unfortunately, it was a tiny little place, and they only had one room with two beds. Jeanie took it, starting to feel pretty exhausted from the trip herself. She helped Donovan to the room and sent him into the bathroom to take a hot shower.

"I don't want to see your face again for at least a half hour, Curtis," she said, knowing he needed to soak his back in order to loosen the knotted muscles.

While he was in the shower she made some phone calls. Twenty minutes later she stuck her head in the door, telling him she'd be back as soon as she could, that he should lie down on the bed after his shower. He groaned in response. She grinned, knowing he hated to be mothered.

She was back an hour later. She had bought dinner, a heating pad, an ice pack, and a cooler full of ice. She also had a bag from a pharmacy.

Donovan looked at it, raising an eyebrow. "What's in there?"

"Flexeril and Vicodin."

"How did you manage that?" he asked, surprised.

"Well," she said, putting down the food and pulling her planner out of her purse, "I happen to have your prescription numbers right here, and I used a little influence and a lot of moxie and got you a refill up here in Podunk."

Donovan grinned. He had to hand it to her—she did know him well enough to know exactly what he needed. She made him eat before he took any meds, but as soon as he'd taken about five bites she handed him a Vicodin and a Flexeril.

"This is going to knock me out," he warned.

"I know."

He took the meds and finished eating. She plugged in the heating pad and put it on one of the beds. "You sleep here," she ordered, pointing to the pad.

"Yes, dear," he said, already sounding tired. He took time out to call Erin, telling her about his back and that they were staying in a hotel. Erin was concerned about his pain, but he told her how Jeanie had managed to "swindle" some drugs for him. Jeanie laughed at that point, and so did Erin. He hung up shortly after. Jeanie did notice that no "I love you"s were said, but she figured that was for her benefit. Donovan was always a gentleman.

That night Jeanie watched him sleep, still feeling incredibly bad for putting him through this. She was determined to help with the driving the rest of the way to San Diego. They were still seven hours away.

The next morning she woke before Donovan did and decided to take a shower. She realized as she started to get up that she was extremely sore. Every movement she made caused more pain. A hot shower would be just the thing. Walking carefully into the bathroom, she went to take off her shirt, yelping as her muscles screamed at her. Her pants took just as much of an effort to remove. By the time she had her clothes off she had to sit on the side of the tub for ten minutes just to recover.

She turned on the shower and got inside, standing under the hot water. She tried to bend down to pick up the soap that was on the side of the tub and found she needed to rest her hand on the upper part of the shower molding. Halfway to the soap, her supporting hand slipped and she banged her cracked ribs against the outcropping of the shower inset. She cried out involuntarily, because the pain was intense.

Donovan was in the bathroom a moment later, having leaped out of bed when he heard her cry out.

"Jay? Are you okay?"

She didn't answer. She was standing under the water crying softly, hurting and feeling horrible all at the same time.

"Jay?" Donovan said again, poking his head behind the shower curtain. He sucked in his breath sharply when he saw the black bruises seemingly all over her body.

She turned her head, having heard his intake of breath.

"Don't look at me," she said, feeling horribly ugly.

"Jay…" he said softly. "Honey, I know what you look like."

"Yes, but right now…" she said, turning away.

A moment later he climbed into the shower behind her, wearing his sweats. He pulled her back against him, holding her. She turned in his arms and let him, feeling the water running down her body. After a while she made him turn around so the hot water would run over his back, because she knew he'd be hurting again. They stood that way for a long, long time. She laughed when she touched the waistband of his sweats.

He helped her wash her hair, and gently washed her back and sides for her, even going down to one knee carefully to wash her legs. Jeanie marveled at the fact that he was doing all this, but nothing sexual was occurring between them. Part of her was astounded at his control, but then her mind told her, *Yeah, it's because he doesn't want you anymore.*

Meanwhile Donovan was thanking the effects of Vicodin and Flexeril for not allowing his body to react normally to the fact that he was touching her again.

After the shower, he helped her out carefully, laughing as his sweats dripped all over the floor. He dried her carefully, wrapping her in the thankfully bathsheet-sized towels. She left the bathroom and Donovan took his shower, washing up. Unfortunately, he had nothing to walk out of the bathroom in other than a towel. He went into the other room with one wrapped around his waist. Jeanie was curled up on the bed watching TV. She looked so tiny in the bathsheet, he couldn't help but grin. Meanwhile she was remembering way too much about Donovan's body to be comfortable. He was standing there in a towel, for God's sake—she could think of a million things she'd like to do at that point. None of which she did. She just lay there, pretending to watch TV. He picked up his shaving kit. She'd noticed that he no longer had the goatee. After shaving he pulled a fresh pair of jeans out of his bag and a clean shirt, going back into the bathroom to dress. He heard Jeanie moving around in the other room and assumed she was getting dressed too.

"Are you decent?" he asked before he walked out.

"Compared to what?" she asked wryly.

He chuckled and came out of the bathroom. She was wearing a T-shirt and sweat-style shorts. He noted that she didn't have a bra on, his eyes going to her nipples. Jeanie caught the look and laughed. "I couldn't get the stupid thing on, okay?" she admitted.

"I could help."

She gave him an amused look. "Donovan, you were good at getting them off, not putting them on."

Donovan laughed. "Good point. Well, you can't go out looking like that, babe."

"Why?" she asked, pushing it.

"Because I'd probably have to shoot someone for attacking you, that's why."

Jeanie nodded. "Some Bible banger on a rampage?"

He grinned. "Or some man with a thing for nipples."

"Yeah, but you—" she started, then shook her head. "Never mind."

"What was that?"

"Oh, nothing," she said, smiling as she stood up.

"Uh-huh," he said, unconvinced.

Jeanie laughed. "How's your back this morning?"

"It's better, thanks. The meds did the trick."

"Good old narcotics, huh?" Jeanie said, grinning.

"Yeah, go figure."

They got their stuff together and headed out, stopping to have breakfast at a small café. Jeanie had pulled on a light jacket, and Donovan thanked her for not causing a riot.

While they were waiting for their food they started talking.

"So what's going on, Jay?" he asked, sipping his coffee.

"What do you mean?" she asked, avoiding the question.

"Come on, I know you were running from something. And I know there was something wrong when you were in San Diego last month." He put his cup down, looking her in the eyes. "What's going on? Talk to me."

Jeanie hesitated for a long moment, not sure she had the right to dump all this on him, but she needed to talk to someone, just to get it out.

"I hate it, Donovan."

"Hate what?"

"All of it. The academy was awful. Most of the guys hate me or want to lay me, or in the case of my partner, both."

"Dominguez?"

She nodded. "The guy at the hospital."

"He didn't seem too pleased to have me there."

"He's been trying to get in my pants since day one."

"And not succeeded?"

"Hell no!" Jeanie said, giving Donovan a sour look.

"I'm sorry, Jay, he just seemed pretty proprietary is all," Donovan said, looking apologetic. "So where the hell was he the other night?" he asked, realizing the guy should have been with her.

Jeanie shook her head. "Flirting with some woman."

"Are you serious?" When she nodded, Donovan's tone dropped to a deadly level. "I'll kill the bastard."

"Easy, Curtis," she said, grinning at him, but her heart had warmed a bit that he still cared enough to even threaten such a thing. Then her expression turned serious. "Donovan, I just want you to know that you were right about everything you said. You told me I needed more street time to hone my skills and learn how to handle situations that came up. You were right. God, you were so right." She indicated the bruises on her face then shook her head. "I was so stupid. I threw everything away with both hands and grabbed for something I hadn't earned. That's what you were trying to tell me when you told me to put in the time, but I wouldn't listen. I'm sorry, Donovan, for everything. I just hope that somehow you and I can manage to be friends again someday. Well," she said, indicating where they were sitting, "we are friends. I can't begin to thank you for coming to my rescue. That's the incredible thing about you—you do things like this, for people like me, who deserve it the least."

"Don't say that, Jay. You were hurt, and your family couldn't be there, so I wanted to be."

"Thank you," she said again, reaching up and touching his cheek.

"You're welcome," he said, grinning as their food arrived.

She told him she intended to do some of the driving that day, and he agreed as long as she felt up to it. They took turns one hour on, one hour off. As they got farther south they were running into rain.

"Jesus, it's May, for God's sake!" Donovan said as they were pelted with hail.

It had become decidedly cold, to the point that Jeanie had changed into sweatpants at the last rest stop. She hadn't had a warm jacket, so he gave her his sweatshirt, which hung down to her knees.

They had just hit The Grapevine, on the north side of Los Angeles, when the rain started really coming down. A CHP officer warned them that there was ice on the road. Jeanie pulled over at the gas station right before The Grapevine started.

"Maybe we should stop for now," she said, having noticed that Donovan was moving rather gingerly when he shifted in his seat. It was four o'clock in the afternoon; they'd been taking it slow and easy, driving with all the rain.

"Yeah, let's head back to Bakersfield, have some dinner and grab a hotel."

They found a hotel, checked in, and went to the room, deciding that sharing was a good idea since Jeanie was likely to wake up sore

111

again the next day. Donovan didn't want her alone and in pain. Donovan stepped out on the balcony to make a call.

He dialed his home number, and Erin answered on the third ring.

"How's everything going?" he asked.

"Fine, Donovan. How's your back doing?" Erin asked, concern already coloring her voice.

"I'm okay. It's a little bit sore, but I'll be alright."

"How's Jeanie?"

"She's a mess. She's bruised up really bad."

"Well, you're probably the best medicine she could get," Erin said, smiling.

"Yeah, I have the soaking wet sweats to prove it."

"What?"

"Never mind," Donovan said, grinning. "Long story, I'll tell you when I get back."

"When will that be?" Erin asked, trying not to sound whiney because she missed him.

"Tomorrow sometime. We got caught by ice on the north side of The Grapevine, of all the stupid things in May."

"Probably just as well. You shouldn't overdo it with your back."

"I know, I know."

They hung up a few minutes later.

He and Jeanie went and had dinner, then came back to the room, sitting on the bed and watching TV. He took a Vicodin, but left off on the Flexeril, not wanting to be too groggy in the morning in case there was still ice on The Grapevine. Jeanie took the Motrin and Codeine the doctor had given her for the pain in her ribs. They both ended up snuggled under the blankets since it was freezing in the room, and the heater seemed to think it was off for the season and refused to warm up. At one point the rain got really loud; Donovan turned down the TV, and they both listened to it hitting the street outside and the roof. It was nice to be inside when such dramatic weather was going on outside.

Jeanie woke in the middle of the night. She realized then that they'd fallen asleep lying right next to each other. Apparently the need for heat had made them move closer together. Donovan's arm was just above her head, on her pillow. His other hand was at her waist. Their bodies were only about three inches from each other. His head was above hers, so his neck was right in front of her. She could smell the Tommy cologne that he wore. She closed her eyes and inhaled deeply, remembering all the nights she'd lain with him, putting her face against his neck just to smell him. He'd teased her many times, telling her that all someone would have to do was buy her a bottle of Tommy and she'd never need him again.

Refusing to stop and consider what she was doing, Jeanie moved closer. She knew it was totally habit when his arm came down and slid under her neck. He stirred, but didn't wake, his hand gripped at her waist. She reveled in the feel of it. She leaned up and pressed her face to his neck, inhaling the scent of him again. When she pulled back, he stirred again and opened his eyes.

Donovan stared down at her for a long moment. When he started to speak, she reached up and put her finger to his lips.

"I know you don't belong to me anymore, Donovan," she said softly. "I just wanted to feel close to you again."

"Jay…" he said quietly, a soft plea in his voice.

"Please don't," she said, dreading that he'd tell her he was in love with Erin. "I already know you're living with Erin, okay? I don't need to know anything else."

"She's living there with me temporarily."

"She is?"

"Yeah." He nodded. "Her husband found her and started threatening her."

"Oh man…" Jeanie said, remembering what Erin had told her about her husband.

"Yeah. So until I know she and Bobby are safe, they're staying with me."

Jeanie smiled. "You are always there for people, aren't you?"

Donovan shrugged. "It's no big deal."

"Donovan, don't make light of it. How many people would take people into their home to help them out?"

"Erin's not just anyone," he said, and Jeanie was sure she was about to hear the words she dreaded. "She's my friend. And she's been there for me through all of this." He said the last indicating himself and Jeanie.

Jeanie nodded, giving a self-deprecating laugh. "Yeah, and I'm the bitch that put you through all of this." Her tone of voice wasn't angry; it was self-loathing.

"Jay, you did what you felt you had to do."

"I went for something I didn't deserve."

"People do it all the time."

"Yeah, well, I did it and hurt you," Jeanie said, looking up at him sadly.

He grinned. "I'll live."

"Ya think?" she replied, grinning too.

"Maybe."

"Well, I know being dumped by me is becoming a regular thing," she said, rolling her eyes.

"You're keeping me humble, that's for sure."

"Oh yeah, that was my intention," she said, shaking her head.

He smiled. "I just knew it."

She grew serious then. "I just don't want you to hate me, Donovan. I know I deserve for you to, but…"

"I don't hate you, Jay. I never could."

"I'd like to try and make it up to you."

"You don't have to."

"I want to."

"Let's just see how things go with you, okay?"

She looked back at him for a long moment, afraid to say anything. Was he saying there was still a chance for her? Or did he just mean as friends? She wanted to ask, but she was afraid to.

"Okay," was her only reply.

They spent the rest of the night lying as they were, and sleeping. Jeanie found that it was nice just to be next to him again. She was learning to appreciate the little things about Donovan Curtis again.

The following day they made it home. Donovan took her by her parents' house, staying with her until she was settled in her old bedroom.

"Are you sure you're going to be okay here alone?" he asked.

"Yeah, I'm okay," she said, reaching up to hug him. "Thank you, Donovan. Thank you for everything."

"You call me if you need anything," he said sternly when they parted.

"Yes, sir," she said, grinning.

"Hey, Dave's wedding is tomorrow. Do you want to go with me and Erin?"

Jeanie bit her lip. "Don't you think she might want you to herself?"

Donovan considered the thought, then shrugged. "I don't know. How about I talk to her about it, and call you tonight?"

"Sounds like a plan."

Not only did Erin agree that Jeanie should go, she also called Jeanie and told her that she needed to come over and have dinner with them that evening. She even volunteered to pick Jeanie up.

When Erin arrived, she was aghast at the bruises on Jeanie's cheek. She stepped forward and hugged her. "I'm so sorry this happened to you."

"Serves me right," Jeanie said.

"Are you nuts?" Erin asked, looking surprised.

"No. But I should have listened to Donovan when he told me I needed more street time. He was so right."

Erin bit her lip, looking at her friend. "I'm sorry you had to find out like that then."

Jeanie laughed. "Yeah, you know me, hard head and all."

They walked out to Erin's car, and after they got in, Erin turned to Jeanie, an earnest look on her face. "I just want you to know, I never went after Donovan. It wasn't like that."

Jeanie shook her head. "I know, Erin. I know that. You aren't that type of person. I was just upset that day. I'm sorry I said what I did to you."

"Donovan was a mess when you left. I don't think he even let you see that."

"No, he didn't. But it doesn't matter—he shouldn't have had to go through that because of me. I deserve to lose him."

"You haven't lost him," Erin said, knowing she was probably messing up her own chances of ever holding on to Donovan. Then again, if she had to lie, cheat, and steal to keep him, then it wasn't meant to be.

Jeanie glanced over at Erin, surprised that she would tell her something so damaging to her own bid for Donovan's affections. She realized then that she had been very right about Erin; she was simply a nice person. She leaned over and hugged her tight.

"Thank you for taking care of him," she whispered.

"I wanted to take care of him," Erin said, sitting back in her seat. "I will tell you that I'm in love with him," she said seriously. "I know it's not mutual—I know he cares about me, but he still loves you." She shrugged. "I won't walk out on him, but if in the end he chooses you, I'll know that it's what was meant to be."

Jeanie shook her head, unable to fathom such a reliance on fate.

But she knew Erin believed that everything worked the way it was meant to; her relationship with Donovan was no different.

They had dinner that night, laughing at Bobby's antics with the spaghetti Donovan had made. They talked about the wedding and caught Jeanie up on how Dave had proposed to Susan, both women making a big deal about how romantic it had been. It was a comfortable night for the three of them.

CHAPTER 4

Stevie was trying to finish up her portion of the physical inventory so she could get off that project too. She was working with Kyle Masterson to check individually assigned firearms, going from unit to unit to make sure that the person listed as having been issued a certain weapon still had that weapon. It was a tedious process, but Midnight had insisted that Kyle accompany Stevie, not wanting a repeat of the Harris incident with any other officer in the department.

During the course of their work, Stevie had a chance to talk to Kyle.

"You're seeing my sister," she said, catching him off guard.

"I know," he replied.

"You know her history?" Stevie asked, her tone no-nonsense.

"Yes, I do."

Stevie nodded, looking straight ahead as they got in the elevator. "Then you know if you hurt her, I'll kill you personally, right?"

Kyle looked over at her, his eyes narrowing at the threat. Then he remembered he was dealing with the young lady who'd gone after a high-level drug dealer singlehandedly because he'd killed her brother-in-law. She might actually mean what she'd said.

"I don't intend to hurt her, Ms. O'Neil," he said after a long silence.

"Good," Stevie said as the elevator doors opened. "Then we should get along just fine."

Kyle stood where he was for a moment, staring after her with a bemused grin on his face. The girl had balls, that was for sure. He had to stop the elevator doors from closing to get out behind her. He smiled to himself, shaking his head. God help the man that screwed with Stevie O'Neil.

Christian Collins was the man that would dare to screw with Stevie O'Neil. They ended up working together the following day, because Kyle was pulled into a last-minute meeting about budgets. Stevie had a meeting with the District Attorney to go over her testimony in the Marco Tiempo case. Later, when she walked into the office, Christian just stared at her openmouthed. She was dressed in a hunter green suit, with the skirt cut a good four inches above her knees. The jacket was tailored perfectly to her petite frame, making the fact that she had a perfect body even more obvious. Under the jacket she wore a beige silk-and-lace camisole with spaghetti straps; when one looked closely enough, it revealed a fair amount of beautifully tanned skin. Her hair was pulled up at the top and fell in rich, fiery waves almost to her waist. She wore silky nylons and hunter green three-inch heels. Her makeup was perfect, her lips a glossy auburn color.

Christian couldn't take his eyes off her, and found that he had the insane desire to take her to a dark corner somewhere and remind her of how much he craved her. But that wasn't possible anymore, he reminded himself; she was now coldly off limits. Overnight she had become the ice queen when it came to him. He still had no clue as to what he'd done to warrant her attitude toward him, and he'd begun to wonder if he ever would.

"Not one word, Collins," she warned, her tone icy, as she noted his stare. "I met with the District Attorney this morning on the Tiempo case."

"When is it?"

She narrowed her eyes at him, but said, "The day after Dave and Susan's wedding."

He held up his hands in surrender and turned his chair back around to face his desk.

Ten minutes later they were set to leave the office. They were going out to one of the task forces with offices in another part of town. Christian drove, opening the door for her as usual. She'd unbuttoned her suit jacket by this time, and he couldn't help but notice the expanse of perfect skin at her shoulders as she moved past him to get into the car. He closed his eyes momentarily, forcing the thoughts out of his head.

Getting in on the driver's side, he started the engine. Halfway to the other office, he couldn't take the silence anymore.

"Am I ever going to know why you're pissed at me?" he asked, hating that he couldn't just let it go.

Stevie looked over at him, as if surprised to find him sitting there next to her. "I don't have a problem with you, Collins. I'm just done."

"Done?" he said, his face indicating he was appalled by the word.

Stevie shrugged, looking back out the front window. "Yeah, monogamy's not really my thing," she said, her tone so off-handed that Christian's hand tightened on the steering wheel as he winced slightly.

Her barb had indeed struck home. Their conversation about

121

only sleeping with each other came back to him in a rush, making him surprisingly angry that she'd used it against him.

"Yeah, me either. Honesty's always been a problem too," he said, his voice a sneer.

His barb struck too. Stevie realized he was telling her that he'd lied when he'd told her she was the only one he was sleeping with. The thought made her sick. She clenched her teeth, then forced herself to relax as she looked back over at him.

"You should be relieved then," she said, her eyes turning to ice. "And quit bitching."

"Done," Christian said, with the finality of a gavel rap.

"Good," was her only reply. They were silent for the rest of the drive.

They spent the day examining weapons for serial numbers, making notes on any discrepancies. They visited three offices, the last of which was a narcotics task force, done in cooperation with the State Bureau of Narcotic Enforcement. They had three PD officers working there. When they walked into the cubicle for the last officer whose weapon they needed to check, there was a second man there, talking to the officer.

Bob Forrester's eyes went to Stevie immediately; she was the kind of woman you didn't miss, with her fiery auburn hair, green eyes, creamy skin, and incredible body. He gave Christian a cursory glance, but his eyes were drawn back to Stevie again. She smiled at him.

Stevie couldn't help but notice Forrester. He was tall, dark, and fairly handsome. He had black hair that went to his shoulders and rich chocolate brown eyes surrounded by long, dark eyelashes. His chiseled features made him seem like a hardened cop, but when he smiled he had perfect white teeth that made him even more catching to the eye.

"Barrows," she said to the other man, much more bland by comparison, who sat at the desk. She knew him from her time at the department.

"That's me," Barrows said, standing up. "How you doing, O'Neil?"

"I'm alright. How's it goin'?" she asked, her eyes trailing back over to Forrester. Christian leaned against the door, noting the play between Stevie and the dark-haired guy, and finding that he didn't like it at all.

"Oh, hey, Forrester, this is Stevie O'Neil," Barrows said politely as he pulled out his gun.

"Clear it, please," Stevie said.

Barrows obligingly released the magazine and cleared the chambered round, locking the slide back, then handed the weapon to Stevie. She held it up to the light to check the serial number—D77098, which she called over her shoulder to Christian. He checked it and nodded.

Stevie looked at Forrester then, extending her hand. "Good to meet you."

Forrester took her proffered hand and shook it, looking at her oddly.

"Stevie O'Neil..." he said. "You wouldn't happen to be Frank O'Neil's daughter, would you?"

Stevie narrowed her eyes, then nodded slowly. "Yeah, I'm Frank

O'Neil's daughter. Why?" she said cautiously.

The man started grinning. "You don't remember me, do you?"

Stevie shook her head slowly. "Should I?"

"I was a rookie under your dad. He was my FTO the year before he died…" He trailed off as she started to nod.

"Okay, yes, I do remember you," she said, smiling. She glanced at Christian and noted the sardonic grin on his lips. "You came to the house a few times—you drove the red Camaro."

Bob laughed, nodding. "You were always into cars, like your dad."

"Yep, and that Camaro was cherry. Whatever happened to it?"

"Wrapped it around a lamp post six years ago," he said, sighing.

Stevie shook her head. "Criminal. You're not still with the department, are you?"

"Nah, I'm over at Narcotic Enforcement now."

"Ah, okay," Stevie said, smiling again.

Bob looked at her for a long moment, then shook his head. "Little Stevie O'Neil…" He trailed off as his eyes slid from her face down her body, then back to her face. "You sure did grow up nice," he said, a serious come-on in his voice. "Damned nice."

Stevie saw Christian tense visibly. She shook her head at him imperceptibly, her green eyes connecting with his. Bob glanced at Christian, but said nothing.

"Well, thanks," Stevie said in answer to his compliment.

Bob stepped closer, rubbing his chin. "So, when are you gonna be done here?" he asked, his voice lowered. "Maybe we can get a drink somewhere and you can tell me how you've been."

"That could take a while…" Stevie said with a sly grin.

"That's okay, I've got all night," Forrester replied, staring back into her eyes.

Stevie was sure Christian was about to come unglued; it made her grin.

She looked at her watch. It was 4:45 already. "I think I can take off now—give me a sec." She turned to Christian, giving him a warning look. "You can finish up here, can't you?"

Christian's face was like stone as he gave her a tight false smile. "Sure, why not?" he said icily.

"Good," Stevie replied, a green fire starting in her eyes.

Meanwhile, the San Diego PD sergeant leaned over and whispered to Forrester, "Careful, she's got a direct line to the chief."

Forrester looked back at his friend, surprised, but nodded.

Stevie turned to Forrester. "Ready?

"Oh yeah," Forrester said with a quick grin.

He led her out to his Grand Prix. Once inside he looked over at her as he started the car, still amazed at how the lanky kid she'd been at ten had turned into such a beautiful woman. "I hear you've got a direct line to the chief—that true?" he asked, grinning at the cliché of office gossip.

"I don't, really," Stevie said, shrugging. "Those guys just think that because the chief reinstated me and gave me a TnD to sergeant."

"Sounds like she likes you."

"I guess."

"So," Bob said as he drove out of the parking lot, "that fairly intense-looking man with you looked pretty unhappy. Did I interfere in something?"

"Nope," Stevie said simply, staring straight ahead, her jaw set.

Bob narrowed his eyes at her. "Why do I get the feeling I'm being used?"

Stevie looked over at him, her green eyes staring right into his. "You're not being used yet. Would you like to be?"

"Ohh..." he said, his voice deep as he grinned. "Now that sounds like an offer."

"Are you going to take all night considering it?"

"No, I can think of better things to do all night," he replied smoothly.

"Good."

To hell with Christian Collins—she was free to do as she pleased. Could she help it if he was hung up on his ex-girlfriend? That was his problem to deal with. She was going on with her life.

The next morning she looked tired, and Christian noticed.

"So, did you fuck him?" he couldn't help but ask.

She looked him right in the eye and said, "All night, as a matter of fact, and this morning too. You want details?"

"No," he said, leaning back in his chair. "I've already been there."

Stevie hid the fact that his comment burned like hell. She turned and sat down in her chair, spinning back around to face him. "You won't have to worry about ever going there again," she said, then turned back to the desk.

It took everything she had to keep the tears of rage and humiliation back. She knew she'd just come off like a whore, but it was better than him knowing the truth—that although Forrester had been an accomplished lover the one time they'd had sex, he wasn't Christian, and that was all she could think the entire time. She'd left Forrester's house two hours after she'd gotten there, going home and lying awake half the night, trying to reason out why she couldn't get over Christian Collins, the bastard.

Christian was doing a lot of hiding of his own. It burned him no end that she'd gone off with that other guy. He didn't know what he'd done to piss Stevie off so much, and the worst part was, she wouldn't even give him the chance to make it right. She'd shut him out totally, and now she was being vicious. For some reason, though, he couldn't bring himself to stay out of her way. As it turned out, Stevie took herself out of his way. After the guns had been inventoried two days later, she told Kyle she wanted off the project, even going to Midnight to tell her that she needed some time off to get her head together. Midnight could sense a lot of tension in the younger woman and agreed to it, giving Stevie two weeks' paid leave.

Christian was stunned when Kyle told him that Stevie had asked to be taken off the project. She'd walked out without a backward glance, and Christian decided it was time to get over Ms. O'Neil in a hurry. He spent the next three nights at the bar, doing what his friend Tara called whoring, every night going home with a different woman, every morning waking up feeling like shit. He spent the weekend drinking, finding the numbing effects of alcohol much more helpful, and he didn't have anything to compare to Stevie on that score.

Kyle was standing staring out his bedroom window, his thoughts miles and years away, when his phone rang. He picked it up, his mind still elsewhere.

"Hello?" he said absently.

"Masterson, it's Stevie O'Neil. I need your help," Stevie said without preamble.

Kyle's mind came back to the present. "O'Neil. Look, it's not a good time, okay?"

"Look, my sister needs you," Stevie said, her tone leaving no room for argument. "So either you want to be there for her or you don't. Which is it?"

Kyle closed his eyes for a moment, fighting the urge to tell Stevie O'Neil where she could get off. Then he realized that she was right—if Stevie was desperate enough to call him, Rhiannon must really be having a hard time.

"Okay," he said after a long pause. "I'll be there."

Stevie nodded and hung up. She paced around, casting glances down the hallway toward her sister's room. She had come by that evening, knowing Rhiannon would be having a rough time; it was the anniversary of Jason's death. She had found her lying on her bed, Jason's badge, still bent at one edge from the car accident, in her hand. Rhiannon was all but comatose. When talking to her hadn't helped, and fighting with her hadn't worked either, Stevie had done the only thing she could think of, and that was to call Kyle Masterson.

She'd seen changes in Rhiannon since she'd begun seeing Masterson, and Stevie hoped against hope that Masterson was what her sister needed right now. It was worth a try anyway.

Kyle arrived at the apartment twenty minutes later. Stevie let him in, noting that he looked like hell too. Was the whole world going to hell?

"She's in her room, down the hall to the left."

Kyle nodded and walked toward Rhiannon's bedroom.

"Masterson," Stevie called after him.

Kyle turned.

"Thanks."

"You're welcome," he replied, then headed on down the hallway.

He knocked lightly on the door.

"Stevie, just leave me alone."

"I would, but my name's not Stevie," Kyle said, poking his head through the doorway. He walked in and stood looking down at her. She was lying on her side, her legs curled under her. She clenched a gold shield in her right hand.

Kyle reached down, uncurling her fingers so he could see the badge.

Rhiannon's eyes followed his actions. "It was Jason's," she explained unnecessarily, tears still on her cheeks, fresh ones starting in her eyes.

Kyle nodded, moving to sit down on the bed, his eyes on her. "Bad day, huh?" he asked softly.

Rhiannon nodded. "Jason died three years ago today."

Kyle went very still, then turned his head to the side as if denying something. "Today?"

"Yes."

"Rhiannon, Barbara died three years ago today."

Rhiannon stared at him as if he'd become transparent. "Are you serious?"

He nodded slowly.

Rhiannon sat up, still looking like she'd seen a ghost. "Oh, Kyle... I'm sorry."

He looked at her for a long moment. "Could I just hold you for a while?" he asked, his voice a quiet plea.

Rhiannon nodded, holding out her arms to him. He pulled her close and moved to sit with his back against her headboard. They sat like that for a long time, neither of them speaking. Rhiannon was the first to talk, her head against his shirt, her fingers plucking at imaginary threads.

"You know, there are so many days when I just don't know if I can do this anymore..." she said, her voice trailing off as she choked back a sob. "When I don't know if I can live without him."

Kyle nodded. "I know. There are days when I can't find my socks, and I actually want to call out and ask her if she knows where they are."

Rhiannon smiled through her tears. "Jason could never find his socks either. He was hopeless like that. One time, we had to wear dress blues, and he couldn't find his tie tack. He spent an hour looking for it, to the point of almost making us late."

"Where did he find it?" Kyle asked, grinning.

"I found it, in his drawer, where it belonged," she said, laughing softly.

Kyle laughed, shaking his head. "Barbara was our organization queen," he said, smiling. "She knew where everything was, all the time." He took a deep breath, blowing it out in a sigh. "There was one time when she lost her wedding ring…"

"She lost it?" Rhiannon asked, glancing up at him.

"Yeah," Kyle said, grinning at the memory. "She had this dish that she always put it in when she took it off. But apparently a towel edge had gotten under it and it had been flipped over when one of the kids grabbed the towel. They righted the dish, but the ring was gone and they didn't know to look for it."

"What happened?"

"Well, she looked everywhere for that thing, ready to kill all of us for losing it. We finally figured out that it had gone down the bathroom sink."

"How did you get it out?"

Kyle grinned. "Well, three hours and two hundred and fifty bucks in plumbing bills later, she had her ring back."

Rhiannon laughed.

They talked for hours, just telling silly anecdotes about their spouses. It felt good to talk about them, but be there together. Just before midnight, Rhiannon looked up at him, concern on her face.

"Where are the boys?" she asked.

"Nick's at the house, keeping an eye on Brenden."

"Are they okay alone there?"

"Yeah, they're okay. Nick is pretty good about watching out for Bren. Besides, Joe's security system is top of the line."

Rhiannon nodded, satisfied that she wasn't keeping him from

his kids.

She dozed off about a half hour later, and Kyle sat there just holding her. He looked down at her in the semi-darkness of the room, reaching out to touch her cheek softly. He looked heavenward then.

"You had yourself one fantastic lady, Jason," he said quietly. "Thank you for letting me borrow her to heal myself."

Eventually he fell asleep too, holding her against him.

Early the next morning, just as the dawn was breaking, Kyle woke still holding Rhiannon. He saw that she was still asleep. Again he felt the need to reach down and smooth his thumb over her cheek. Her eyes fluttered open just then, and she looked up at him.

"Good morning," he said quietly.

She smiled softly, glancing at the clock. "You should call the boys."

Kyle nodded, grinning at the same time. He liked that she was concerned about his sons. She handed him the phone. Kyle dialed and talked to Nick, who told him he would get Brenden ready for school and out to the bus on time. Kyle thanked his son for his help. "Just make sure the house is locked up when you leave," he cautioned.

"Okay, Dad, no prob."

"Thanks, Nick. I love you," Kyle said sincerely.

"Love you too. Bye." Nick said, and hung up.

Kyle found Rhiannon smiling up at him. "What?"

She shook her head. "I just find it really sweet that you tell your son you love him. A lot of men wouldn't do that."

"Ever since I lost Barbara, I tell them all the time. You know?" he said, knowing she'd understand. She nodded; she did indeed.

"It must be hard on you, raising them alone."

Kyle shrugged. "It has its moments, but I just do what I can." He moved around a bit, wincing.

"What is it?" she asked.

"I'm old," he said, grinning.

She smiled. "Stop that. You're probably just stiff from sitting up all night."

"Yeah, that's it," he said, moving to lie down and pulling her with him. "You know, I think we need a day off," he said, smiling mischievously.

"You mean another day off?"

"Oh, were you off yesterday?"

"Yes."

"Me too," he said, grinning unrepentantly.

"Yes, but we made it through," she pointed out, her voice softening.

"Yes, we did. And you know, I can't help but think that's what was meant to happen, Rhian."

She nodded seriously. "Thank you for that. I know you were probably in your own private hell, but you left it to come save me from mine."

"Did I save you?" he asked softly.

"Yes, you did," she replied, staring up into his eyes.

He kissed her softly on the lips. Finding that he didn't want to pull away just yet, he kissed her again, sliding his hand up her back to caress her neck. Her hands touched his chest tentatively. He pulled her closer as he deepened the kiss. She clutched at his shirt, her lips responding to the pressure of his. When he finally pulled back, he looked down at her. Her eyes searched his, her hands still curled around the material of his shirt. Without a word she moved forward, pressing her lips to his again. They kissed for what seemed like hours. Her hands eventually moved to touch his face, his hair, and over his shoulders.

When they pulled back for a few moments, they were both breathing heavily. He hugged her to him, pressing his lips against her hair. His breath was warm against it. "Rhian, I need you," he said softly. "God, I need you…"

She raised her head and looked up at him. The sun was shining through the windows behind her, and his green eyes, framed in black lashes, just stared into her soul. And she knew she needed him too, that it was time. Rhiannon didn't speak. She simply reached up, touching his cheek, stroking it softly, then moved her lips to his again, kissing him with the hunger he had started in her. His hands slid around her again, pulling her closer to him, touching her, caressing her. He sat up, pulling her gently with him. He unbuttoned the long shirt she wore, then moved to his own buttons, but he found he just wanted to touch her. He slid his hands over her skin, shuddering when she finished opening the buttons he'd started on, pulling his shirt open and touching his bare chest. It took every ounce of control he had, but he took his time, kissing her, caressing her. She did the same to him. Neither of them wanted this to be some carnal union; it meant too much to both of them to be that.

When his body finally slid inside hers, she moaned, looking up at him. He gazed down at her for a long moment, leaning down to kiss her again. Then they were making love, their bodies taking what they had been missing out on for three years. When they reached their climax together, Kyle buried his face in her hair, kissing her neck and saying her name over and over again. She held on to him, her lips pressed against the hollow between his shoulder and his neck, one hand in his hair, the other on his shoulder.

They lay quietly together for a long time afterward. At one point, he moved to the side, taking his weight off her and pulling her to him. She buried her face against his chest. After a while he could feel the tears she was shedding. He kissed her temple.

"Did the guilt just kick in?" he asked softly.

She nodded. He kissed her again, nodding as he did.

After a few minutes she raised her head, looking at him. "I'm sorry, Kyle," she said softly.

"Why?"

"Crying isn't exactly—" she began, but he shook his head.

"Rhian, don't be sorry. We both know that it's going to take time. We never fell out of love with them. It's terrifying to make love to someone else now."

She looked into his eyes and saw that he knew exactly how she felt. She nodded, lowering her head and kissing his shoulder, lying her head back against him.

They lay together for over an hour, each thinking their own thoughts. He stroked her shoulder absently.

"I think we need to play hooky today too," he said finally.

"And do what?" she asked, propping herself up on one elbow to

135

look at him.

He smiled. "I want to show you something."

"And what is that?"

"It's a surprise," he said, grinning mischievously.

The surprise was the '56 Chevy that he'd finally had shipped from New York. He took her for a drive in the country. They walked in fields of wild flowers and through the trees, talking about anything and everything. They stopped and kissed a few times. It was a very relaxing day for them both. He took her to an early dinner at a roadside café. Finally, he drove her back to her house, saying that he needed to get home to the boys.

He was lying in his bed that night at 9:30, resting on his stomach with his arms under the pillow beneath his head. He had one arm extended, his fingers tapping on the nightstand next to the bed in indecision. Just then there was a knock on his door.

"Yeah?" he called.

Nick opened the door. "Dad, there's a lady here to see you."

Kyle turned over, and there stood Rhiannon. He glanced at his son. "Thanks, Nick."

He moved to sit up. "Hi."

"Hi," she replied, with a shy smile. She walked in and sat down on the bed.

"So what are you doing here?" he asked, grinning in spite of himself.

She bit her lip, looking embarrassed. "I just... kinda..."

Kyle smiled at her. "Go on."

"Well, remember when you were a teenager, and you discovered new things... and you just wanted to do them all the time?"

"You want another ride in my Chevy," he said, giving her an all-knowing look.

She laughed. "Yeah. Yeah, that's it."

He leaned over, kissing her lips, then pulled back. "I was just lying there trying to think of an excuse to call you."

"You were?" she asked, grinning like a schoolgirl.

"Yeah. I missed you too."

She leaned against him. "We're pretty hopeless, huh?"

"Pretty hopeless," he agreed, reaching up to hold her against him.

He kissed her softly. She stretched her arms up to encircle his neck as she kissed him back, then snuggled against his neck.

"Kyle, is this going to bother the boys?"

Kyle smiled, loving that she was concerned for his children. It said a lot about her. "Well, Brenden is asleep already and Nick just snuck out of the house..."

"He snuck out?" Rhiannon asked, alarmed.

"Oh yeah, he does almost every night," Kyle said mildly.

"And that doesn't bother you?"

Kyle shrugged. "I know where he goes, and I have patrol keeping an eye on him. He mostly hangs out at the beach with some kids. I figure if he feels like he's getting some freedom, he might not feel like he needs to rebel more."

Rhiannon looked up at him. "Don't you think it would be better to let him know that you know what he's doing?"

"Why do you say that?" he asked, interested in her opinion.

She moved to sit up, as did Kyle. "Well, he thinks he's getting away with something right now. He thinks he's pulling one over on you."

Kyle nodded. "Okay…"

"So he's basically stealing his freedom. Whereas if you tell him you know he's been sneaking and exactly what he's been doing, then give him permission to go out at night, then you're *giving* freedom."

Kyle thought about it. "Don't you think it'll lose its allure then? The whole sneaking out thing is more fun than Dad saying he can go."

Rhiannon shrugged. "Okay, but if it loses its allure, you don't lose anything, and your son gains more respect for you because you are aware of what he does."

"So he'll be less likely to try it again, or something else," Kyle said, giving her an amazed look. "How do you know so much about raising kids?"

"I know what Stevie was like to try and keep in line."

Kyle laughed. "I can only imagine."

"Oh, you have no idea the heartburn that girl gave me."

"You forget, I've met your sister."

Rhiannon laughed. "True."

"You're right, though. I've been letting him get away with too much lately, thinking that if I just give him some rein he'll feel less smothered."

"Yes, but sometimes less smothered is read as less loved."

Kyle kissed her on the lips. "Thank you."

"For?"

"For helping me see things a little more clearly."

"Any time," she said, smiling up at him.

He lay back, pulling her down with him. They lay together for a long time, not speaking, just enjoying being near each other. She touched her lips against his neck, then moved her head from side to side, her lips brushing over his skin, then kissed him again.

Kyle made an "mmm" sound in his throat, his hand at her waist tightening. He reached over with his other hand and raised her face to his, kissing her lips tenderly at first, then deepening it as he pulled her closer to him, then over him. They kissed forever, taking it slow and enjoying each other. When they made love it was with more intensity, taking more time in their new comfort with each other. Afterward there were no tears, only a quiet sense of belonging to each other.

"Rhian..." he said softly, caressing her as she still lay over him.

"Yes?" she replied, her voice right next to his ear, her cheek resting on his shoulder as she faced him.

Kyle hesitated for a long few moments. "Would you think I'm crazy if I told you that I think I'm falling in love with you?"

She moved back, looking up at him. "No, I wouldn't."

He turned onto his side, moving her so they faced each other.

"It's crazy—it's like we were meant to be here together," he said, searching her eyes. "I've been so dead inside for so long, but it's like you've lit me up again." He shook his head. "I guess the only way I

139

can describe it is that I'm falling in love with you."

She nodded. "I know what you mean. It seems like that's got to be impossible, after all we've lost... but it's not, because I feel the same way about you. Last night when you came to the house, I knew Stevie had called you, because I know how she does things. But then you told me about Barbara and I just knew... I knew that you were the one to take my heart again."

"I love you, Rhiannon," he said, staring into her eyes.

"And I love you, Kyle Masterson."

They kissed for a long time, then just held each other, feeling like life was finally beginning again. They knew there would be things to overcome, but they'd do it, because life mattered again.

"So, you want to go to a wedding tomorrow?" he asked, kissing her temple.

"Dave and Susan's wedding?"

"Yeah."

"I wasn't going to," she said, moving to kiss his shoulder again. "I thought it would just make me feel worse right now... but now, I think that yes, I'd like to go."

"Good," he said, grinning. "Now I have a date."

She laughed softly. "Yes, Chief, you have a date."

They got up after that. Rhiannon got dressed and Kyle put his sweatpants back on, both worried that one of the boys might come in. Kyle sat back down on the bed and watched Rhiannon as she brushed her hair out at his bathroom sink. He smiled, enjoying the sight of her. She turned and saw him looking at her, and smiled at him too. He held his hand out to her and she walked over to him, sitting down on the bed. He pulled her into his arms. They sat that way for a long while.

The doorbell rang then, and Kyle glanced over at the clock on the nightstand. "Oh shit."

"Nick?"

"Probably," Kyle said, getting up. He went to the front door, and Rhiannon walked into the living room, wanting to stay out of the way.

Kyle opened the door to two patrol officers and his son.

"Good evening, Chief Masterson," one of the officers said, nodding to Kyle.

"Good evening," Kyle replied, staring at his son. Nick wouldn't look at him. "What's going on, guys?"

"Well, we, uh, caught your son drinking this evening," the second officer said.

Kyle narrowed his eyes at Nick. "Is that so?"

"Yes, sir," the first officer said.

"Well, thanks for bringing him home. I'll take care of it from here," Kyle said, his tone darkening as his eyes bored into his son's downcast face.

"You have a good night, sir," the first officer said, thinking he knew exactly what Kyle was going through; he had a sixteen-year-old who was going through the rebellious stage too.

The officers walked away, and Kyle opened the front door wider to admit his son. Nick didn't move.

"Nicholas?" Kyle said sternly.

Nick looked up at his father. "Is she still here?" he asked, still not making a move to come into the house.

Kyle looked back at him for a long moment, realizing that Rhiannon's concern hadn't been unfounded. He nodded slowly. "Yes, she's still here."

"You're fucking her, aren't you?"

"Nicholas Alexander Masterson!" Kyle shouted, stunned by his son's venom as well as the language he'd used. "If you have a problem with me that's one thing, but I will not have you talking like some punk off the street. You've been raised better than that." He stepped back, opening the door wider. "Get in here and go into the study. I'll deal with you in a minute." There was no arguing with his tone now, and Nick knew better than to challenge him any further. He stepped into the house and headed toward the study.

Kyle watched him go, shaking his head, not sure what he was going to do. He knew he'd wanted to hit his son a minute ago when he'd spoken like that, and he'd never wanted to strike Nick before.

"Kyle?" Rhiannon asked, standing in the doorway to the living room.

Kyle looked at her, blowing his breath out. "What am I going to do?"

Rhiannon walked over to him, reaching up to smooth his brow. "He needs reassurance right now. He thinks you're forgetting his mother. He needs to know you love him and that you're worried about him."

Kyle looked down at her for a long moment, not sure what he'd done to deserve an angel like her to save him from his trials, but he was damned glad he had her. He kissed her softly on the lips. "Don't go anywhere."

"Are you sure?" Rhiannon said, looking worried. "Kyle, maybe you need to take the time to—"

"No. I'm going to talk to him, but I'll be damned if he's going to make my life into a shrine to his mother and make me suffer forever. I need you, and whether he realizes it or not, in being good for me, you're good for him."

Rhiannon smiled. "Okay, I'll wait in the living room. Go talk to your son."

He kissed her again and hugged her. Then he walked toward the study, taking a deep breath and blowing it out slowly. When he entered the room, Nick was sitting in the chair, his feet up on the desk, looking for all intents and purposes like the rebellious youth.

Kyle walked over and leaned against the desk, looking down at his son. "Okay, let's hear it. What's going on with you?"

Nick was silent for a minute, his face set in a stubborn line. Then he looked at his father. "Who is she, Dad?"

Kyle was surprised at the question, but nodded. "Her name is Rhiannon Templeton. She works at the department with me." When Nick said nothing, looking like he was waiting for more, Kyle continued, "She's been helping me deal with losing your mother. She lost her husband three years ago yesterday too."

Nick looked surprised at that, but didn't comment on it. "And you're sleeping with her," he said matter-of-factly.

Kyle took a deep breath, annoyed at having to answer to a fifteen-year-old about his sex life, but then nodded.

"You're forgetting Mom, aren't you?" Nick said, his tone less hostile this time.

"Nothing and no one could make me forget your mother. And Rhiannon's not trying to make me forget her. Do you know what we spent the day today doing?"

"What?" Nick asked, his tone indicating he already knew.

"We spent it talking about your mom and about her husband."

"You did?" Nick still sounded unconvinced.

"Yeah. I told her about the time your mom lost her ring down the sink." Kyle grinned. "And about the time she poured bleach on her plant, thinking it was water, and killed the thing, and how we taped the leaves back on to try and make her feel better. Do you remember that?"

Nick grinned. "Yeah, she thought we were nuts."

"Yeah, I think she accused us of plant abuse," Kyle said, chuckling.

"Well, you told her she'd committed herbicide," Nick reminded him.

Kyle laughed, nodding. Then he looked at his son seriously. "Nick, I'll never forget your mom. She meant the whole world to me. But the fact is, she's gone, and nothing I do can bring her back. I was dying inside, and being dead inside means I can't feel anything, and that takes away from what I can give you and Bren. I know your mother wouldn't want that. She loved you boys more than anything, and she'd want you loved with all my heart. But a heart that's dead can't love, Nick. Do you understand?"

Nick looked at his father for a long moment, then nodded slowly. "And this woman helps that?"

"Yes, she does. But not because of sex," Kyle said, his voice soft and pleading. "Sex is just something that happens when you feel so much for someone that you need to feel closer to them. I've told you that. Rhiannon makes me feel alive again. She's been through hell in losing her husband, because she loved him so much. And she's surviving too. She's been living the half-life I have for three years too. When she and I talk, we're able to remember the good things about the people we loved, and we're able to share things about ourselves with each other. And it feels good, because I'm connecting with someone again. Does that make sense?"

"I guess so," Nick said, struggling to understand. He had noticed a difference in his father lately; he'd been smiling more, playing more with Brenden and joking again. Maybe this woman was the reason for that.

"Now," Kyle said, his voice become stern. "About this drinking. Why were you doing it, Nick?" When Nick didn't answer him, he continued, "Was it because you were angry about Rhiannon? Were you trying to hurt yourself or me?"

"How would it hurt you?" Nick asked, once again looking rebellious.

Kyle looked back at his son for a long moment, then shook his head slowly as if not believing he could ask that question. "When a person drinks they lose their inhibitions, they lose their reasoning. Suddenly things that they wouldn't normally even think of doing, they think might be kind of cool. Like driving, or fighting with some guy, or having sex unprotected. It stops you from thinking clearly." Kyle pinned his son with a serious look. "If something ever happened to you, Nick... I don't know what I'd do. You're my son, my flesh and blood. Your mother and I created you out of the love we had for each other. I love you more than my own life. Don't you know that?"

Nick looked back at his father, surprised. His dad had always said "I love you," but it just seemed so hollow most of the time, at least to Nick. But maybe it really wasn't.

"I guess I did it to hurt you," he said honestly.

Kyle nodded. "Do me a favor, okay?"

"What?"

"If you want to hurt me, hit me, call me names, yell at me, whatever you have to do." Kyle shook his head. "But please, Nick, don't hurt yourself to hurt me."

"If I hit you, you'd bust my ass."

Kyle inclined his head. "That's the consequences of your actions, but at least you wouldn't be doing something where I couldn't watch out for you."

"And that's your job," Nick said, mirroring the words his father always said.

"And that's my job," Kyle agreed with a smile.

Nick thought about it for a long minute then nodded. "Okay, Dad. Can I meet this woman?"

"Sure, if you want to." Kyle went over to the door and called out to Rhiannon.

She came in a few moments later, looking at Nick, who stood and walked over to her.

"Nick, this is Rhiannon," Kyle said, his hand on her waist.

Nick looked at her, realizing she really was pretty. He extended his hand to her formally, and Rhiannon smiled as she took it.

"Your father has told me a lot about you, Nick," she said.

"Well, you can like me in spite of that," Nick said, Kyle's quick wit coming through.

Rhiannon laughed. "I think that just might be possible."

"I'm sorry to hear about your husband," Nick said, surprising Kyle with the sudden maturity.

Rhiannon looked into Nick's eyes, seeing the sincerity there. "Thank you," she said softly.

Nick nodded. He looked at Kyle. "I think I'm gonna go to bed now. Is that okay?"

"Sure."

"It was nice meeting you," Nick told Rhiannon.

She smiled at him. "It was nice meeting you too, Nick."

Nick left the room. Rhiannon and Kyle looked at each other. Kyle blew his breath out slowly. "I have to hand it to you, Rhian—you had it nailed."

"He was worried about you replacing Barbara?"

"Yeah."

"But you explained it to him?"

"Yes, I did."

"And you apparently told him about Jason too."

"In trying to explain our connection, yes," Kyle said. "I hope that doesn't bother you," he added cautiously.

"No, it doesn't bother me. I was just surprised, is all."

Kyle nodded, leaning against the closed door. "I want them to know you. I also want them to understand that you're important to me."

Rhiannon nodded. "Thank you for that."

"Hey, no problem," he said, grinning.

"Your son has your wit."

Kyle grimaced. "Oh yeah, my rebellious streak and wild side, too."

"He's a boy, Kyle—all boys have a wild side. And rebellion is part of life. It's what defines who we are."

"How'd you get so smart?" he asked, smiling fondly.

She grinned. "Practice."

He hugged her. "I think I could use you around here a lot more."

Rhiannon smiled, snuggling in his embrace, happy to be there.

***

Dave hadn't seen Stevie for a week and a half. He'd heard from Joe that Christian and Stevie were on the outs. He mentioned it to Susan that night as they lay in bed.

"They broke up?" she asked.

"I don't think they were ever officially a couple, honey."

"David, she's in love with him. I know she is."

"Well, if she is, she sure isn't acting like it. Joe said she's asked to be pulled from every assignment that has anything to do with Christian."

"You should talk to her, see what's going on." Susan was concerned. Stevie had been very kind to her, giving her advice that had ended up making a change to her life.

"I will soon," he said, lying back and pulling her against him, kissing her softly on the lips.

The following day, he got a phone call from Stevie; she'd left a message on the answering machine.

"Hey, Dave, it's me, Stevie. Look, I don't think I'm going to make it to your wedding tomorrow. I'm sorry, but… I just… I can't make it, okay? But you two have a good time, and a great honeymoon, okay? Talk to you soon."

Dave listened to the message twice that evening, stunned. Susan listened to it with her mother when they got home from shopping.

"David," Susan said, looking worried now, "you need to go talk to her."

Dave nodded, still looking astounded. "Yeah, I think you're right," he said, concern creeping into his voice. He'd heard from Midnight that day that Stevie had requested two weeks off to "get her head together." There was definitely something up.

It had taken some time to run down Stevie's new address, but he'd gotten it. He knocked on her door at 8:30 that night. She answered out of breath; she'd been doing kickboxing to work off some of her tension.

"What are you doing here?" she asked, walking over and picking up a bottle of water. "Aren't you getting married, like, tomorrow?"

Dave leaned back against the door, legs crossed at the ankles, arms over his chest. "Yeah, I am, and I want to know why one of my best friends isn't going to be there."

Stevie looked back at him for a long moment, then dropped her eyes from his. She shrugged nonchalantly. "I just can't make it."

Dave nodded, then pinned her with a look. "I need you there, Steve."

She looked back at him for a long moment, her eyes searching his, then shook her head. "No, you don't. You don't need anyone there, Dave. You'd marry Susan on the moon if that's what you had to do."

He narrowed his blue eyes at her, seeing that she was evading. "Okay," he acquiesced. "I want you there."

"I'm sorry," she said, sitting down heavily on her couch, staring at the floor.

"No, you're scared," he said, pushing off the door and walking toward her. He knelt in front of her, catching her eyes with his. "What happened, Steve?"

She looked away from him, making a show of rubbing the sweat off her chin with her sweatshirt.

Dave reached up, turning her face back to his with a fingertip. "What happened?"

She tightened her lips as she looked away from him again, tears shining in her eyes suddenly even as she shook her head.

"Steve, come on."

"It doesn't matter, Dave, okay?"

"It matters. What happened?"

"I was stupid," she said, her voice shaky. Her eyes were narrowed in self-directed anger.

"How were you stupid?" Dave asked. When she wouldn't answer, he said, "Was it Blue?"

"No, it was me."

"How, Steve?"

She looked at him then, her green eyes showing him how much she was hurting. "Because I was stupid enough to think that maybe he'd gotten over the woman you're marrying tomorrow." With that said she broke down, choking back sobs as Dave pulled her into his arms.

"What happened? What did he say?" he asked as he stroked her back.

She shook her head. "Nothing," she said, her voice muffled because her face was buried in his shirt. "He didn't say anything, he just... He still loves her, and it was so obvious and... I just can't believe I let myself do this." She cried harder then, hating herself more for breaking down, but she blurted the story out anyway. "He disappeared the day you asked Susan to marry you, and I found him—he was at a bar, drunk off his ass. And I got him back to his place, and he... I touched him and he just jerked away from me, and when he looked at me, Dave, he was so devastated. He'd lost the woman he loved, and I was just some sloppy fucking second. I can't believe I was so fucking dumb." She took short, gasping breaths as she felt the pain come back. "God, this hurts. It fucking hurts so much. I hate this."

Dave held her close, rocking her. He didn't have a clue as to what to say. He knew Christian had always said that if he ever married anyone it would be Susan. Susan had told him that. He also knew Christian had always considered Susan his territory. It was possible that Christian was still harboring feelings for Susan; there had never been a complete break with him. Now he didn't have any idea what he could say to Stevie to make her feel better. But he knew for a fact that running was only going to make her feel worse.

"Steve, you have to come to the wedding."

"No, he'll be there—I can't." She shook her head. "No."

"You can't run from him. I doubt you've ever run from anything in your life for long. Don't start now, babe."

Dave stayed with Stevie for two hours, finally getting her to agree to come to the wedding. Eventually she told him to go home to Susan.

At the front door he turned to her. "You're going to come, right?"

"Yes," she said, still not looking happy about the prospect.

"If I have to I'll come over here and get you."

"Knock it off, Dibbins. You're the groom—it's your job to say the 'I do,' not come after me. I'll be there."

"Good." He leaned down to kiss her on the cheek.

"Dave?" she said as he turned to leave.

"Yeah?"

"Thanks."

He grinned. "Any time. See you tomorrow."

"Yeah, yeah, get out of here," she said, shooing him out the door.

That night she went to bed and cried for a good long time, finally allowing herself to feel all the hurt she had inside, hoping that doing so would make her stronger the next day when she had to face Christian again.

Susan woke on her wedding day to the feeling of Dave's lips kissing her softly on the cheek. She opened her eyes to look into his.

"Good morning," she said.

"Good morning," he replied, kissing her again.

She glanced at the clock; it was 5 a.m.

"You're not..." she began disbelievingly.

He nodded, grinning.

"David, it's our wedding day!" she exclaimed, smiling in spite of herself.

He gave her a lopsided grin. "I know, and I need to get myself together mentally."

"Are you having second thoughts?" she asked, her voice holding a hint of concern.

"No way," he said, without hesitation.

"But you're going surfing to get yourself together mentally?"

"Yes," he said, leaning down to kiss her lips.

"Can I go with you?"

"You'd do that?" he asked, surprised.

"I want to share everything in your life, including that which you enjoy the most," she said, her voice mildly chiding.

"Well, that's been reprioritized now," he said, his grin mischievous.

"It has?" Susan asked, totally in the dark.

"Yeah," he said, caressing her skin and kissing her deeply. "I have something I enjoy more than surfing now."

"Oh…" she murmured against his lips. "Then stay here and do that."

His laugh was warm, and he kissed her again, taking the time to make love to her. At 6:30 they got up together, took a shower, and headed for the beach. She sat on the sand, watching him surf, enjoying the way he looked riding the waves that crashed onto the beach. She couldn't believe how much she loved him, and that in a few hours she would be his wife. After a while he came out of the ocean, his surfboard under one arm, his eyes on her. He tossed the board down on the sand next to her and lay down on it, looking up at her.

"All mentally together now?" she asked, smiling.

"Oh yeah." He smiled happily. "But I think I'm going to either have to start waking up earlier or going to work later."

She grinned. "Why's that?"

He levered himself up to sitting, reaching over to touch her lips with his still-wet finger. She kissed it, tasting the salt from the ocean.

"Because I have to manage to make love to my *wife* and surf every morning if I'm going to remain this happy."

"I like that…" she said, brushing a lock of wet hair off his forehead.

"Which part?"

"The part where you said 'my wife.' Although the other part

sounds pretty intriguing as well."

"I hope so," he said, grinning.

"Count on it, Mr. Dibbins."

"I'll do that, Mrs. Dibbins."

After a while they got up and walked hand in hand back to his car. He put on his shorts over his wetsuit and then opened the door for her.

"Ready to start this day?" he asked.

"Very much so."

Six hours later, Susan was sure she was going to go crazy before this wedding was over. She had purposely kept the guests to a minimum, inviting only her and Dave's closest friends and her parents, sister, and grandparents. The list totaled just fifty people.

They were getting married on the beach beside the jetty in front of the Hotel Del Coronado, and the reception was taking place in one of the ballrooms inside the hotel. Dave had insisted that they have the reception somewhere nice. Susan had been aghast at the price of the room, since Dave was paying for it. He hadn't batted an eyelash when she quoted it to him. He'd only said, "Do you like the room?" She'd nodded, and he'd added, "Then rent it."

He'd been incredibly sweet about the entire wedding planning. Originally he joked, saying, "Just tell me where to show up," but when it came down to it, if she was unsure of anything, they talked about it and came to a decision together. He usually deferred to her tastes, however, citing his lack of knowledge on such subjects. One particularly amusing incident was when Deborah had insisted that they needed to register for wedding gifts.

"What are we going to register for?" he asked, leaning back on the couch, his long legs stretched out, his feet up on the coffee table.

"Well, you register for things like china and crystal," Deborah said.

"China?"

"Yes," Susan put in. "The pattern you want."

Dave had looked at her for a long moment. "I don't know anything about china, hon."

"So I guess asking you about crystal is pointless, right?" she replied, grinning.

"Only if you're talking about crystal meth, honey. I'm an expert on that."

"Oh lord," Susan said, rolling her eyes and laughing.

Sitting in the room having her hair done that day, she was smiling, thinking about the conversation. It just seemed like everything was taking forever. She found that, like Dave, she just wanted to get married; she didn't care how anymore.

Meanwhile, Dave was standing in Joe's kitchen with Spider, Joe, Rick, Kana, and Midnight. They were drinking shots.

"I still don't believe it," Spider said.

Dave grinned. "Believe it."

"You better take care of my niece," Rick said.

"I plan to."

"And you better not make her quit working," Joe said, narrowing his eyes at Dave.

"Yeah right, like she would."

"You can't even stop smiling, can you?" Midnight observed, very happy for her friend.

"Nope."

"Don't fuck up," Kana said with a straight face, then started to smile when everyone stopped dead for a minute.

Everyone laughed.

CHAPTER 5

The guests were seated, waiting for the wedding to begin. Dave and Spider walked out wearing charcoal-gray tails, with distinguished-looking striped cravats at their throats. They waited in front of the gazebo that had been set up for the wedding, draped in sterling silver roses. "You ready for this?" Spider asked.

"Man, I've been ready for this my whole life," Dave said, smiling broadly, his blue eyes shining as the music began.

Katherine Sinclair walked down the long, white-clothed aisle, wearing a dress of ivory lace and ivory sandals. From a basket she dropped lavender and purple rose petals. She stopped and mugged for the cameraman, eliciting chuckles from the guests.

"That's Sinclair blood there," Rick said, getting a laugh from everyone around him, including Joe, who sat next to him.

JT came down the aisle next. He wore a miniature set of tails. He looked very mature and almost regal as he carried the ring pillow. The pillow didn't actually contain the rings; Dave couldn't wear a wedding band because of his undercover status, and he had Susan's ring safely in his pocket, refusing to let her see it until he put it on her finger during the ceremony. When Joseph Thomas Sinclair stopped for the cameraman, he lifted his chin slightly, staring directly into the camera, all blue eyes and pride.

"Now *that* is Sinclair blood," Joe said, and again everyone laughed.

Midnight was Susan's matron of honor. She came down the aisle wearing a black silk dress that nipped in at her slim waist then flared to fall two inches above her knees. Her jewelry, a teardrop necklace, earrings, and a bracelet, were the deepest amethyst. Susan had given her them as a gift the night before.

When Midnight stopped for the cameraman, Rick spoke up. "Now *that* belongs to me," he said seriously and with a great deal of pride. Midnight's smile was brilliant as she winked at him. The wink was captured on film. Midnight grinned at Dave as she moved to her place to await Susan's entrance.

Meanwhile, an extremely nervous Susan was standing in the area that had been closed off for the wedding party. Her father had been "unable to attend." After agonizing over it for days, she'd decided to give herself away.

"I'm an adult. I can give myself to you in marriage," she'd said reasonably. Dave hadn't commented.

She stood peeking out to watch the procession. She was a vision of casual elegance in a silken lace dress with a sweetheart neckline that skimmed her small waist and hips, flaring slightly to fall to her ankles. Her hair fell in a cascade of honey-colored curls, tendrils of which were arranged around her wreath-style headpiece, woven with baby's breath and tiny purple flowers. She held in her hands an arrangement of sterling silver roses, white roses, and white lilies that cascaded from her hands. Christian stared at her for a full minute before she turned and caught a glimpse of him standing there.

"Christian?" she queried, her tone worried. She wasn't sure why he wasn't sitting with the rest of the guests, and his presence at this time worried her. Certainly he wasn't going to attempt to repeat the scenario from her last wedding. This time it was different; she wanted to marry Dave more than anything. Even if that meant hurting Christian to do it. She hadn't been sure he'd even come. But here he was, looking very shady in his long coat. "What are you doing here?" she whispered as he walked up to her.

He looked at her for a long moment, his light blue eyes searching hers. "Just wanted to see if you're still going through with this."

"Yes, Christian, I am."

"Do you love him beyond all reason, Zan?" he said, the same question he'd asked her three years before when she was preparing to marry Warren.

"Yes, more than anything," Susan replied without hesitation.

"And he makes you happy?"

"Yes, very happy."

Again his blue eyes searched hers. Then he reached up, undoing the buttons on his coat. To her utter shock he wore gray tails, exactly the same as Dave's and Spider's.

"Then let's go get you married," he said, taking her hand in his. He leaned down to kiss her softly on the cheek, then put her hand on his arm. "I'm giving you away," he said as the music started for her to walk down the aisle. "Dave asked if I wanted the job."

She stared up at him openmouthed for a long moment, then nodded as her smile started. Dave had disappeared a couple of nights before, saying he had something to take care of. She was sure this was that something.

She was right; Dave had gone to Christian's place at Joe's house to ask him. He'd basically come right to the point.

"I want to know if you'd like the honor of giving Susan away at the wedding."

Christian had been stunned at first. "She know about this?"

"Nope. But I think it's only right that the man who helped bring out the woman that she is today gives her to me for the rest of her life."

Christian had been moved by the statement, and he'd known then beyond a shadow of a doubt that Dave loved Susan the way she deserved to be loved. He'd just wanted to be sure of her love for Dave. He was now, and he was proud to give her away at her wedding.

Everyone was stunned when Christian Collins escorted Susan Endicott down the aisle, handing her over to Dave with a very sweet kiss to her cheek. Dave and Christian shook hands, their eyes meeting for a moment. Christian inclined his head to Dave in a rare show of respect. It was a poignant moment that left many of the guests, who knew the history of this situation, feeling awed. Stevie, who sat at the back with Kyle and Rhiannon, did her best not to pay any attention, but she felt a lump in her throat that she couldn't seem to get rid of.

The wedding was presided over by the chaplain for the San Diego Police Department, who Dave and Susan had decided on as generally safe religion-wise. He gave his speech about being gathered here to join this man and this woman in holy matrimony. When the time came for the vows, however, Dave and Susan took over. Dave had told Susan that whatever else they did, he wanted to have their vows be their own, no one else's. Susan had been surprised at the request and also very happy at the prospect of being able to say what she wanted to in front of God and everyone.

They turned to each other. He smiled down at her, his blue eyes shining bright. "You look so beautiful," he whispered.

She smiled at him brilliantly as the chaplain explained to the guests that Dave and Susan had decided to create their own vows. Then it was time for them to begin.

Susan looked up at Dave, her sapphire blue eyes connecting directly with his. "I love you for all the words you say. I love you for all the words you don't say. I love that you don't correct me when I call you a name that no one else, not even your mother, uses." She paused as a chuckle ran through the guests, and Dave laughed softly, shaking his head. "I love that you wake up in a good mood every morning. I love that you always tell me where it hurts and that you'll let me make it hurt less. I want to take care of you when you're sick, feed you when you're hungry, make you smile when you're down, and laugh when you're angry. Most of all, I just want to love you for the very special man that you are, and for everything you bring out in me." She took the chain and cross that he'd given to her and held it up to him. He looked down at her for a long moment, then bent so she could lift the cross over his head and place it back around his neck. "I give you back your symbol of independence, and take from you only your love."

When she finished she had tears in her eyes. He reached up and touched her cheek softly, smiling at her, his own eyes misting.

"When I was a young boy," he said, staring into her eyes, "and things would get bad in my life, I'd jump on my bike and ride the two miles to the beach. By the time I'd get there, I'd be so hot I'd jump off the bike and dive into the water. I'd swim until I was exhausted, then get out, almost blue from the cold ocean water. I'd climb up onto this rock I'd claimed as my own and lie in the summer sun. I'd let the sun warm my blood and heal my hurts." He touched her cheek again.

"You are the sun to me now. You take me in and heal my soul with your warmth. I love you for that, and I will love you for the rest of my days." With that he pulled out the ring he'd bought her.

Instead of the wedding band she'd expected him to place on her finger, it was a band and ring set of white gold, with nine small round diamonds and two marquisette-cut deep blue sapphires. In the center was a large round diamond. Susan drew in her breath at the beauty of the ring, lifting her blue eyes, exactly the color of the sapphires, to Dave. "Oh, David…" she said, her reaction telling him everything that she thought without words. He smiled at her, very glad she liked his choice.

The ceremony proceeded and the chaplain pronounced them man and wife, telling Dave he could kiss the bride. The guests watched breathlessly as Dave touched Susan's cheek, trailing his hand down to her jaw, lifting her face to his, and kissed her so tenderly there was no mistaking his deep love for her, if there had still been any doubt in anyone's mind. Everyone cheered as Dave deepened the kiss, pulling her close. Both Dave and Susan broke into laughter as someone issued a catcall.

Dave sat comfortably on the wide windowsill in the lounge, his long legs bent at the knees, his back against the side of the sill. He stared down at the ocean, his mind drifting back over the wedding ceremony. He didn't hear the door open, so he didn't see his bride watching him.

Susan stood looking at the man she'd just married. She had been so astonished at his vows, that he had said what he had. The words had made her feel more special than she ever had in her life, and she had no words to describe the way she felt at that moment. One's wedding day was purportedly one of the most stressful days of a person's life. Yet there her husband sat, calm as you please, looking like a big cat sitting on the windowsill, watching the world outside.

She walked over to him, and he turned when he sensed her there. His blue eyes twinkled as he smiled at her. She touched his cheek. "Thank you for the incredibly thoughtful words…" she said, trailing off as he slid down from the sill, coming to stand in front of her.

"I meant every one of them," he said softly. "I liked what you said too, and it's exactly what I need from you—but you know that, don't you?"

"Yes," she said, nodding. "I love you, David."

"I love you too," he said, staring down into her eyes. He pulled her into his embrace, kissing her softly. "You look so beautiful to-day."

She smiled. "And you look very handsome. I don't suppose I can get you into a tuxedo more often, can I?"

Dave laughed. "I doubt it, honey."

"Then I'd better enjoy this. By the way," she said, her face growing more serious. "Thank you for what you did. With Christian and all."

Dave nodded. "I just thought it seemed right."

"Well, I think a few people were rather shocked."

"Good," he replied, grinning.

"Well, it certainly showed everyone what kind of man you are."

"What kind of man is that?"

"David, you had my ex-boyfriend, who most of those people witnessed taking me out of my last wedding, give me to you. It shows everyone how much confidence you have in our relationship, that you're that secure."

Dave grinned. "Well, I didn't mean to do all that. I just thought you'd feel better with an escort, and I figured since he's the one that brought you out of your cocoon, he should be the one to set you free."

Susan looked at him for a long moment, then shook her head slowly in amazement.

"Uh-oh," he said, giving her a serious look. "What did I do this time?"

"You just astound me sometimes. The way you say things to me…" She shook her head again. "You always make me feel so special."

"That's because you are, Susan. Don't ever believe anything else."

"With you by my side, how could I?"

"That's the plan," he said, grinning.

Just then, Spider knocked and walked in. "You two ready to be presented to the world?"

Dave and Susan looked at each other. "Think we could just hide out in the room upstairs?" Dave asked, with a twinkle in his eye.

"We could…" Susan said, grinning at him.

"Bullshit, we have some serious partying to do," Spider said, making them laugh.

"Then carry on, man," Dave said, and gestured toward the door. He took Susan's hand and followed Spider toward the reception hall.

Dave and Susan entered the room to applause. They walked

around talking to everyone. Dave made a point of going over to Stevie first. She looked sedate in a green lace peasant-style dress—sedate but beautiful.

Dave hugged her. "How you doin'?" he asked quietly.

"I'm okay," she said, looking very subdued. She smiled and hugged Susan. "You two looked great."

"I owe you my thanks," Susan said.

"Yeah," Dave said, grinning. "I hear if it wasn't for your excellent 'kick Dave in the ass' advice, we probably wouldn't be here right now."

"Well, you did need a good kick in the ass," Stevie said, laughing. "But that's not what I told her."

"You told me not to let him go," Susan said, holding Dave's arm. "And I don't intend to, ever."

Stevie looked closer at Susan's hand, examining the ring. "Oh, Dave... nice choice," she said, whistling appreciatively.

Dave grinned. "As long as she likes it, I'm happy."

"I love it," Susan assured him.

Midnight motioned to Susan then, so she excused herself to go to her aunt.

"So how much did that cost ya?" Stevie asked conspiratorially.

"Enough," Dave answered as he started to walk away.

"Dave!" Stevie called after him.

He turned around and held up four fingers. She started coughing, then laughed. She went in search of Rhiannon and Kyle then, finding them at one of the tables. She saw Christian across the room;

he was impossible to miss, his black hair standing out against the gray tails. She'd managed to avoid him so far, but she found she couldn't keep her eyes off him. It annoyed her no end.

After a while the DJ called for the happy couple's first dance. Some were surprised by the choice of song; others weren't. Moody Blues' "Nights in White Satin" was a classic rock song, but the words were very poignant. Dave sang them to her as they danced. Everyone looked on, smiling. Susan was busy being surprised at what a nice singing voice her new husband had.

"You never told me how beautifully you sing," she said during an instrumental part.

He grinned. "Oh, you'll find I'm full of surprises, honey."

"I can't wait to discover all your hidden talents," she said earnestly.

"Oh, how I love you…" he sang, leaning down to kiss her deeply.

At their table, Kyle and Rhiannon watched. "I love this song," she said, smiling.

"Me too," Kyle said, then narrowed his eyes. "If you tell me this was yours and Jason's song, I'm leaving now."

"Why?" she asked, glancing at him. "Was it yours and Barb's?"

"Yes," he said seriously.

"Well, no, it wasn't Jason's and mine, but we both really liked it."

"Whew," Kyle said, wiping his brow comically. "I was getting nervous for a minute there."

She smiled. "Too creepy, huh?"

"Oh yeah," he said, taking her hand, not caring who saw or what they said.

Rick noticed, nudging Midnight and motioning discreetly with his head. She looked over to where Kyle and Rhiannon sat and saw their clasped hands. She smiled, nodding. She was happy that they seemed to have found each other. She glanced at Rick and saw him looking rather serious for a moment.

"Hey," she said, nudging him. "I love you."

He looked down at her and smiled as he put his arm around her, pulling her close, bending down to whisper in her ear, "I love you, more than you'll ever understand." He kissed her cheek, then turned her face to his and kissed her lips.

"Break it up," Joe said as he walked by.

"Drop dead, Sinclair," Rick said.

Joe grinned. "No, that was weeks ago."

"Shut up!" Midnight whacked Joe on the arm and gave Rick a dirty look as he laughed. "You two are hopeless," she said, starting to walk away. Rick grabbed her hand and tugged her back to him, pulling her close and kissing her again. She smiled up at him, and Joe went back over to the table where Randy sat.

He sat down, kissing her on the shoulder as he did. She smiled. "Harassing Rick again?"

"Always," Joe said, grinning unrepentantly. He kissed her lips, his hand sliding under her hair to hold her there.

"Break it up," Rick murmured as he and Midnight walked by. Joe laughed, as did Randy.

Erin watched them from the other side of the table, finding it very romantic. She'd been in love with Joe and Randy's story since Randy had told it to her.

"You still here?" Donovan asked, leaning over and whispering in her ear.

"Where would I be?"

Donovan grinned. "Oh, off on some distant continent with some white knight."

She smiled. "Only if he has sandy-brown hair and teal-blue eyes."

"Oh," he said, smiling. "We have that kind of knight here on this continent."

"Really?" she asked, looking surprised.

"Yeah," he said, leaning down to kiss her on the lips. "Surprisingly close by."

"I'll take him."

"Yeah, but where?"

"Oh, pretty much anywhere," Erin said, grinning. "The couch sounds good."

Donovan laughed, shaking his head. "We'll just see about that."

"Oh goody," she said, smiling angelically.

"What's goin' on here?" Jeanie asked as she walked back to the table.

She'd been over talking to Christian. He'd been concerned about the bruises he'd seen even though she'd tried to disguise them with makeup. He'd been extremely pleased to hear that the guy he'd decked in San Francisco had been the partner that allowed her to be alone long enough to be hurt. "Serves the bastard right," he'd growled.

Jeanie sat down in the chair next to Donovan and reached over, taking a drink of his beer.

"I can get you one if you want one," Donovan said.

"Would you?"

Donovan stood up. "You got it." He looked at Erin. "You want anything?"

She smiled. "No, I'm fine, thanks."

Donovan went over to the bar, where Christian stood leaning against the wall, having just finished a shot; he was now drinking his third beer. Donovan ordered beers for himself and Jeanie, then two shots of Jack Daniels. He turned and handed one to Christian.

"What's this for?" Christian asked.

Donovan grinned. ' For decking Frank Dominguez in San Francisco."

"I'll drink to that," Christian said, knocking back the shot and chasing it with another gulp of beer.

"I know you didn't know who you were decking, but thanks anyway," Donovan said after drinking his shot. He extended his hand to Christian.

"No problem," Christian said, shaking Donovan's hand and nodding.

Donovan walked away, carrying the beers. Christian scanned the room until he saw Stevie. He was fighting every urge he had to go over and talk to her. Dave came over to the bar then.

"Hey, Blue," he said, glancing at the younger man.

"Hey, Dave."

Dave ordered a Jack and Coke, with a shot on the side. He downed the shot then took his drink. He turned to Christian, noting the direction he was looking in, right at Stevie.

"I talked to Stevie," Dave said.

"Yeah?" Christian said, trying to look disinterested.

"Yeah." Dave leaned against the wall next to him. "You messed up," he said calmly. Christian turned his head sharply in surprise. Dave looked back at him for a moment, his eyes searching Christian's face, then he turned back toward Stevie. "I don't think you did it on purpose," he continued. "I don't think you even know what you did."

"I have no clue," Christian said, being honest.

Dave nodded. "Ask my wife to dance."

"What?" Christian asked, confused now.

"Just do it, Collins, and trust me."

"Okay…" Christian said, setting his beer down and pushing off the wall, shaking his head as he walked off across the room toward Susan. He touched her on the waist. "Your husband wants me to dance with you," he said quietly.

Susan looked up at him, her eyebrows furrowed. She glanced over his shoulder to locate Dave, and saw that he had just left the DJ and was headed for Stevie. She grinned, realizing Dave was doing something to solve this problem between Stevie and Christian. She wasn't sure what, but she walked with Christian to the dance floor.

Dave came up behind Stevie, who'd been purposely turned away from the bar area because she knew that was exactly where Christian was.

"Dance with me," he murmured, taking her hand and leaving her no real choice. He led her to the dance floor and turned her around before she could see Christian was there too.

Stevie looked up at him, and he could see that she was miserable. "Saw Blue over at the bar," he said conversationally.

"So?" she replied icily.

Dave shrugged. "He's drinking pretty heavily."

"Good. I hope he has a big fat headache tomorrow."

Dave shook his head at her maliciousness. "Wouldn't kill you to talk to him, you know."

"Bullshit."

The song they were dancing to ended, and another began. Dave had asked the DJ to play another slow song, and he put on the latest Darren Hayes. "Insatiable" throbbed from the speakers.

Dave turned and, still holding Stevie's hand, walked over to Christian and Susan.

"I'd like to dance with my wife," he said, grinning down at Susan.

Christian released Susan, stepping back. Stevie stood staring openmouthed at Christian as Dave took his wife in his arms and moved off. Without a word he reached out and took her hand, pulling her to him.

"God," she said through clenched teeth. "Please don't make a scene here."

He put his lips to her ear. "Then dance with me. That's all I want."

Stevie shuddered at the feeling of his voice so close to her again. He felt it, but was wise enough not to comment. He held her in his arms, moving to the music. Stevie could smell his cologne, Havana; he had told her while they were in San Francisco, when she'd asked. He smelled so good, it made her mind go back to the thoughts of that night at the club. She closed her eyes and let go of her anger for just a few minutes. Without realizing it, she leaned against him, and he moved his hand up her back to hold her to him. Christian was reveling in the feel of her again. It was insane to need one woman so much—he knew it.

All too soon the song ended, and the spell was broken. She stepped back, narrowing her eyes up at him as if indeed wondering what kind of spell he'd tried to put on her.

"Stevie…" Christian began, taking a step toward her.

Her hand came up, staving him off. "No," she said, turning and walking away. She went straight over to Dave, who was talking to Spider. She stood on her tiptoes and kissed him on the cheek. "Thanks, but I'm outta here," she said, then walked away.

"What?" Dave said. He stared after her, then glanced at Christian, who was watching her leave too. Christian turned to Dave and nodded, then strode after Stevie.

Stevie was in her car by the time Christian got to the parking lot. She sped past him.

"Damnit!" he yelled, then strode to his car, pulling off the cravat as he started it up and followed her. He unbuttoned his collar as he drove, cussing all the way. Bloody woman wouldn't even listen to him!

Stevie noticed that he was following her two lights later. It was hard to miss the sapphire blue Dodge Viper. "Damn him!" she growled. When the light changed she shot through it and threw on all the speed she could manage. Unfortunately for her, the Viper had a much more powerful engine, so Christian kept up with her easily.

When she got to her apartment, she parked on the street, getting out and glaring at him as he did the same.

"What the fuck is wrong with you, Collins? Can't you just leave me alone?"

Christian strode up to her, his light blue eyes blazing at her, mad that she'd almost managed to kill herself a few times just to evade him. "No, I can't."

With that he reached out and, putting his hand behind her neck, pulled her to him, kissing her hungrily. To his shock, she bit his lip and pulled away, then punched him in the jaw. Jesus! She could hit! He fell back a bit, stunned that she'd actually punched him, but he saw that she was striding away. He stood there debating the sanity of going after her again. She wasn't carrying, but…

His thoughts trailed off as he noticed the dark sedan that had slowed down just behind and to the right of her. Christian started running even before he saw the muzzle of an AK47 poked out the window.

"Stevie!" he yelled just as the gunfire started.

He was two feet away when the first bullet struck her, and still the shots continued, hitting her again and again. Christian dove for her, knocking her to the ground and covering her. He cried out as a bullet slammed into his shoulder, and covered his head and hers. Then he heard the squeal of tires as the car took off.

"Jesus, Jesus…" he chanted as he moved off her. He turned her over carefully. There was blood everywhere. "Shit!" he said, tears of rage blinding him.

He grabbed her purse, dumping the contents on the ground and grabbing up her cell phone. He dialed 911 and told the operator to get an ambulance there now. He had to look for the address; fortunately it was on a sign ten feet from him. He dropped the phone, trying to figure out where all she was hit. Stevie didn't move or make a sound.

"Please don't do this, please…" he said as he tried to apply pressure to the wounds he had found, but there was no stopping the blood. She was bleeding to death, and there was nothing he could do. She lay in his lap, a limp rag doll.

"Stevie, goddamnit, no!" he yelled as people started coming out of their apartments. Someone handed him a towel, and he used it to try and stop the blood. He cried out as someone pressed a cloth to his own bleeding shoulder.

When the ambulance arrived the paramedics took over, putting Stevie on a gurney and rushing her to the ambulance. Christian rode with her, holding her lifeless hand. He prayed for the first time in his life during that ride. Once at the hospital, they hurried her into emergency surgery. Christian stood in the emergency room just staring at the door they'd taken her through. Was that the last time he'd see her?

He stumbled over to a pay phone, searching his pockets for change. Finally he found enough to make a call. He dialed information and had them put him through to San Diego PD dispatch. He told the dispatcher his name and that she needed to page the chief and Assistant Chief, that one of their officers was down and at Mercy Hospital. He hung up and sank to his knees, leaning his head against the wall and staring unseeing ahead.

Susan's was the next voice he heard.

"Oh my God! Christian!" she said, seeing the blood now clotting at his shoulder. Dave moved to help him up, and sat him down in the nearest chair. Christian looked up. Joe, Midnight, Randy, and Rick were there too.

"What happened?" Joe asked.

Christian shook his head. "Not me..." he said hoarsely. "Stevie... Stevie was shot..."

"Oh my God," Midnight said. "I'll go page Kyle."

"They're on their way," Donovan said as he, Erin, and Jeanie came through the doors.

"It's Stevie that was shot," Midnight told him.

"Shit," Donovan said, turning around. "I'll go rush them."

"What happened?" Joe repeated.

Christian shook his head slowly, his mind numb. "It was a dark sedan... dark gray... Cutlass... late model." He closed his eyes as a wave of nausea hit him, swallowing against it. "Didn't get the plate. Had to have been Tiempo—she was testifying tomorrow." He breathed heavily, trying not to pass out.

Midnight looked over at Dave. "You know Tiempo almost as well as Stevie."

"I know him better," Rhiannon said from behind them, her eyes lit with green fire. "That bastard has screwed with my family one too many times."

"Okay, let's get on it," Midnight said, her tone all business. "I want that bastard in cuffs or a box in the next five hours."

"You got it, Chief," Dave said, his face set in a determined line. "I'll grab Spider on his way in. Joe, Rick, you coming?"

"Oh yeah," Joe said. Rick nodded.

"I'm coming too," Midnight said.

Christian got to his feet. "I'm going with you."

"You've already been through too much," Midnight said, shaking her head. None of them had realized he was actually injured too. They all assumed the blood was Stevie's.

"They just shot my lady. I'm going, and I'm going to beat the shit out of someone," he said, his voice stronger now.

Midnight nodded. She turned to Susan. "Will you stay and wait for the doctor to tell us how she's doing?"

"Yes," Susan said, nodding.

"I'll stay too," Erin said, stepping to her side.

Midnight nodded. "Thanks, Erin."

The group turned and walked toward the doors. Dave stayed behind, looking down at Susan. "You gonna be okay?" he asked, worried that she looked so pale.

"I'm alright, David," she assured him. "I love you. Be careful."

"I'm always careful, honey," he said, hugging her to him. "We'll pick up our wedding night here later, okay?"

She glanced up at him and caught his quick grin. She kissed him, and then he was gone.

Susan turned back to Erin, who just shook her head.

Both women sat waiting to hear how Stevie O'Neil was doing.

Meanwhile, Stevie O'Neil was fighting for her life. She'd been hit three times by fire from an AK47 rifle. There was damage to her body that the doctors did everything they could to correct. One round was lodged against her spine, having ripped through her mid-section. They didn't remove it, only repairing the damage it had caused. The bullet was lodged in such a way that taking it out could cause her permanent paralysis—if she even lived through the night. Two doctors worked on her for eight hours, finally closing her up and hoping for the best. She'd lost a great deal of blood, almost two-thirds of her body's capacity.

The team, including Joe, Rick, Midnight, Dave, Kana, Spider, Tiny, Donovan, Christian, Rhiannon, Kyle, and Jeanie, who had included herself, hit the house they'd worked out was where Tiempo's people were hiding, thanks to Dave's informants, who had been threatened with various painful injuries if they didn't give them up. Christian went after the man they knew to be the shooter, grabbing him by the throat and punching him in the face, then dragging him up and punching him again. Finally he beat the man into unconsciousness, while Joe, Spider, Dave, and Rick stood with their backs turned, their weapons at the ready.

Joe glanced over his shoulder. "Done?"

Christian looked up at his cousin from his place over the man's body. It didn't look like he was done.

"We can't let you kill him, ya know," Joe said.

Christian stood up. "Then I'm done."

With that, Dave hauled up the unconscious man and dragged

him to the paddy wagon waiting outside. Christian staggered over to a nearby wall, leaning against it, fighting waves of dizziness. He'd changed out of his tails into raid gear, managing to keep everyone from seeing the damage to his shoulder. Beating the man had hurt like hell, but he'd drawn on his anger and the adrenaline pumping through his veins. Unfortunately, that was wearing off fast.

"Man, I need to get back to the hospital," he told Joe. "I want to see how she is."

Joe nodded. "Rhiannon and Kyle already took off. Go with Rick and Midnight."

Christian nodded. He followed Rick and Midnight out to Rick's Mustang, stumbling a few times but catching himself before he fell. Fortunately neither of them noticed. He climbed into the back and rested his head against the back of the seat. He must have lost consciousness at one point, because suddenly they were at the hospital. He climbed out and went inside with Rick and Midnight.

"How is she?" he asked as he walked up.

Rhiannon turned to him. "They don't know yet. They're still working on her."

"Jesus…" Christian said as he moved to sit down. He rested his head against the wall, closing his eyes again. The hours ticked by.

He either slept or passed out, because when he woke Susan was sitting next to him, Dave on her other side. He looked around; the entire group was there. He knew they hadn't heard anything yet, because everyone still looked up with anticipation every time a doctor came out of the OR. Finally one called out, "Stevie O'Neil?"

Rhiannon jumped up, Kyle right behind her. "That's my sister," she said. "How is she?" Her eyes begged the man not to say the words she'd heard too many times in her life—the "We did everything we could, I'm sorry" speech.

The doctor looked back at the young woman. "I'm Doctor Tim Procter. Your sister has sustained three gunshots. There was a lot of internal damage. We've done everything we can to repair the most critical of her injuries. She's lost a great deal of blood. She's in a very critical condition at this point. I'm sorry, I wish I had better news."

Rhiannon just stared at the man. Kyle held her, his arms around her shoulders. She nodded numbly to the doctor. "Can I see her?" she asked softly, trying desperately to hold back her tears.

The doctor shook his head. "Not right now. I'll let you know when you can." He walked away, not liking the looks he was getting from many of the people standing around him.

"Christian!" Susan screamed as she saw him fall. Joe and Dave reacted fast enough to catch him before he hit the floor.

"He's out cold," Joe said, checking his cousin.

"David!" Susan exclaimed.

Dave's head snapped up, and he saw that she was pointing to the wall where Christian had been leaning. There was a trail of blood that led to a small pool below.

"He's been hit!" Dave yelled. "Get a doctor now!"

Joe checked his body and found the wound in his shoulder. "Jesus, this is an AK round! He must have been hit in the initial assault."

"What the fuck was he doing on the raid then?" Spider asked.

"Getting revenge," Dave said, moving to pick Christian up. Joe helped him. A gurney and a doctor arrived and they took Christian away.

Joe paced in agitation. "This just keeps getting worse," he muttered angrily. Midnight nodded, looking at Rick. He just shook his head.

When Christian woke up, he was lying in a hospital bed. Susan was standing next to him.

"How is she?" he asked, his voice still hoarse.

"The same," Susan said softly.

Christian closed his eyes for a moment, then moved to get up.

"Christian, you can't get up!" she exclaimed, pushing him back down.

"I can't just lie here, Zan," he said harshly.

"You're hurt—you have to rest!"

"I'm fine," he said, starting to sit up again, pushing her hand away.

"Hey, watch how you treat my wife," Dave said from the doorway. He grinned. "Stay down, man. You can't be any use to her if you pass out again."

Christian dropped his head back against the pillows, shaking it. "Fuck. If I'd just been faster…"

"If you'd been faster, you'd be fighting for your life right now," Dave said.

"Better me than her," Christian countered.

Dave had no reply to that. "Look, just rest. You did everything you could. Now we have to let fate do its job."

Christian said nothing, looking out the window.

Christian spent exactly one day in bed "recovering," then he was up and out in the waiting room with everyone else. He was told by Joe to go back to recovery; he was ordered by Midnight, begged by Susan, and threatened by Spider and Tiny. Nothing worked. He sat firmly in the waiting room with the rest of them. Susan finally gave in and brought him some food, harassing him until he ate. Dave watched his wife with a grin.

It was six days before Stevie awoke the first time. They'd all taken to staying at the hospital in shifts, except Christian and Rhiannon, who stayed every day, all day and night. Kyle was there as often as he could be, but needed to be home with the boys at some points too. He sat Brenden and Nicholas down one evening and explained to them that Rhiannon's sister had been hurt badly and that was why he needed to be at the hospital so much. On the third night, Nick suggested that Kyle take them with him, so he could stay longer.

Kyle walked into the waiting room with his two boys. He introduced Brenden to Rhiannon. Kyle was proud of Nick, who was respectful and expressed his sympathies for Rhiannon's sister. Rhiannon smiled softly at the young version of Kyle. Brenden looked at her for a long time, and then to Kyle's surprise, climbed up into her lap and touched her cheek, telling her, "It'll be okay," mirroring what Kyle always said to him when he was hurt.

Rhiannon looked up at Kyle with tears in her eyes, and he nodded, moving to sit next to her and hold her hand. Brenden stayed in her lap for a long time, somehow sensing that she needed the support.

Christian sat on the waiting room couch, alternately sleeping on it when he couldn't keep his eyes open anymore. Susan, Jeanie, and even Erin tried to get him to eat and drink as often as possible, but he really wasn't interested. His shoulder was aching constantly. The doctor told him he needed to have another exploratory surgery, that perhaps they had missed some shards of bone when they'd done the original. Christian refused to let them.

They'd let Rhiannon into Stevie's room a few times, but Stevie had remained unconscious and they had shooed Rhiannon out, worrying about germs and things.

Stevie awoke slowly, emerging from a haze. She glanced around, not sure why she was there. Then the pain hit her, and she groaned softly. Looking above her, she saw the nurses' call button. She reached for it, gasping as the pain intensified. She depressed the button then lay back, panting from the effort.

The nurse saw the call light go on and jumped up from her station to run down the hall. Christian's eyes followed the woman and he stood up, as did Rhiannon. Then the nurse was yelling down the hall to the other nurse to get Dr. Procter. Rhiannon and Christian started moving at the same time. Dave, who was there with Susan, stood up too and started moving down the hallway.

When Rhiannon walked into the room, Stevie was panting and writhing around. Rhiannon stepped to the side of the bed, reaching down to touch her sister's forehead.

"Stevie, honey, I'm here. It's okay," she said soothingly.

"It hurts," Stevie said, her voice so small and childlike.

"I know, honey. I know," Rhiannon said. "They're getting the doctor right now, just hold on." She looked over at Christian, who was standing in the doorway. He walked in, moving to the other side of the bed.

"Stevie, listen to me," he said authoritatively. "Look at me.

183

You're going to be okay. Just hold on, babe." He took her hand and she squeezed tight. She looked back at him, but her eyes were glazed over in pain. There were tears streaming down her cheeks.

She shook her head, shaking as the pain seemed to worsen. She tensed and cried out. Dave moved to her side.

"Steve, listen to me!" he said as he reached down, turning her face toward him. "Breathe, babe, you gotta breathe. Slow... Take a slow breath, and breathe it out. You can do this, Steve." His voice became a soothing chant. "Breathe, baby... breathe. Slow... slow. You can do this. It's okay... you're okay. Breathe..."

Stevie seemed to relax some then. Rhiannon and Christian sighed with relief. The doctor arrived, ordered morphine for her IV, then went to the other side of the bed to check her vital signs. Dave kept her attention on him.

"Don't worry about that, babe. Just breathe. You're gonna be okay. It's okay. Breathe..." he said over and over again, his voice smooth and soft. The nurse added the morphine to Stevie's IV, and within minutes her eyelids drooped as the medication kicked in and took away the pain. A couple of minutes later she was unconscious again.

"We're going to need a decision here," the doctor said. "Her vitals are good right now, but it's obvious that we're either going to have to take that bullet out or shore it up. She's in an extreme amount of pain, and that's going to hinder her progress."

"I can't make that decision for her," Rhiannon said, having already talked to their mother, who was far too frail to be there at the hospital all the time. "She'll need to decide."

The doctor nodded. "But she'll have to have it explained to her.

She needs to understand that even the surgery could paralyze her. I want her to understand the risks. If we shore the area around the bullet up, she could live a normal life without too much hindrance. She'd have to be careful though."

"She wouldn't be able to be in law enforcement anymore," Dave said, looking over at Rhiannon. They both knew that was what Stevie lived for.

Rhiannon nodded, looking very unhappy. Christian said nothing. He didn't want Stevie risking another surgery, but knew it wasn't his place to speak.

When Stevie woke again, she was dosed heavily with painkillers. Rhiannon was there to explain about the surgery. Christian stood in the doorway, his head back against the doorjamb as he listened to the options, none of which were good.

"I want it out," Stevie said, panting for breath even with a few simple words.

Rhiannon nodded, catching the horrified look on Christian's face.

"Stevie, are you nuts?" he said, moving to stand at the foot of the bed. "Did you hear the part about how taking the bullet out could paralyze you?"

Stevie looked back at him, her eyes narrowed. "No, I heard the part," she said, gasping as she clenched her hand around a fistful of sheets. "Where they said if I don't get it out..." Again she paused to gasp for breath. "I don't get to be a cop." She said the last as if it were a death sentence.

"There's more to life than being a cop," Christian said quietly, his light blue eyes pleading with her.

"Not for me," she replied coldly.

Christian stared back at her, noting the ice in her eyes. He closed his eyes for a moment, then turned and walked out of the room.

Stevie looked over at Rhiannon. "Schedule the surgery, and keep him out of here," she said, then closed her eyes.

Rhiannon was surprised by the ice in her sister's voice. She wasn't sure what was going on, but she did know that Stevie's wish had been expressed. She contacted the doctor and scheduled the surgery.

Stevie went back into the OR three hours later.

She woke the following day. Rhiannon sat next to her. Stevie lay on her side, facing Rhiannon.

"Hi, baby girl," Rhiannon said, reverting to the nickname she'd had for Stevie when they were young.

"Hi," Stevie said weakly.

"The doctor said they think the procedure went well."

Stevie nodded.

It was four more days before Stevie could carry on even the slightest conversation without gasping for air. By then everyone had been in to see her. Everyone except Christian; she'd refused to allow him back into the room. Rhiannon told him about Stevie's edict, her tone of voice indicating that she wasn't very pleased with her sister's attitude. Christian nodded, his light blue eyes reflecting no emotion. But he continued to stay in the waiting room. He had a fever by that time, and was guessing correctly that his shoulder was infected. He refused to address the issue. He still hadn't consented to having another surgery.

Susan was getting extremely worried about him. She'd heard that Stevie wouldn't even see him, and she'd talked to Dave about it. They'd put their honeymoon off until they knew Stevie was going to be okay.

"He's not well, David. I know it—I know him," she said that night when she saw Christian sleeping on the couch. He went home every day long enough to shower and change, then came back to the hospital.

Dave shook his head. "No, he's not well. But he's not willing to do a damned thing right now." He glanced down the hall, toward Stevie's room. "Damned O'Neil is more stubborn than Midnight ever was."

"Can you try to talk to her?" Susan asked.

"I have tried. She shuts me down every time."

Susan sighed. "Something needs to be done. He's going to be deathly ill if he doesn't get some medical treatment soon."

"Some sleep in a real bed and a decent meal wouldn't hurt him either," Kyle said, having been listening to their conversation from his place sitting across from them. "I'll talk to Rhian—maybe she can talk some sense into Stevie."

Dave nodded. "Might work."

Kyle talked to Rhiannon when she came out of Stevie's room an hour later. Rhiannon agreed to try and talk to Stevie.

When Stevie woke that evening, Rhiannon was sitting next to her bed.

"You still here?" Stevie asked weakly.

"Yep," Rhiannon said, smiling at her sister.

"Don't you have, like, a life or something?" Stevie asked, a shadow of her former humor returning.

"Not till you get out of this place, I don't," Rhiannon said seriously.

Stevie nodded.

"Stevie, I need you to do me a big favor."

"What?" Stevie asked, mystified. What could she do right now?

"I need you to talk to Blue."

"No," Stevie replied instantly, her face becoming closed off.

"He's sick," Rhiannon said. "He needs to get some medical attention, but he won't, because of you."

"Medical attention?"

"Yes," Rhiannon said, seeing the sudden worry in Stevie's eyes.

"What for?"

"For the fourth bullet that didn't kill you," Rhiannon said matter-of-factly. "The one that ripped his shoulder apart."

Stevie stared back at her sister for a long moment, then closed her eyes. "I didn't know he was hit," she whispered.

"He was, Stevie. He was hit with an AK47 rifle round," Rhiannon said, her tone sharpening. "And even so, he went on the raid to get the guys that shot you. And from what I hear, beat the living shit out of the man that pulled the trigger, probably doing a lot more damage to his injured shoulder." Rhiannon's voice held no room for argument.

Stevie nodded slowly. "Okay, Rhi, okay." It was obvious she was holding back tears now. "I'll see him. I'll talk to him."

Stevie slept for a little while then. When she awoke, Christian was sitting in the chair next to her bed. His head was bowed, his forearms braced on his knees.

"Christian?" she whispered softly.

His head came up, and she could see how exhausted he was. She could also see the pain he was in. She reached out, touching his cheek. His eyes closed slowly in reaction. When he opened them, he leaned forward, reaching up to brush her hair back from her face, his expression cautious.

"I'm sorry," she said softly.

"For what?"

"I didn't know you were hit. I didn't know…" she said, trailing off as he shook his head.

"It's okay. I'm okay."

"No, Christian, you're not."

"I don't care about that," he said, his light blue eyes searching hers. "You were lying there bleeding to death in my arms, and I couldn't do a damned thing. And…" He took a deep breath, shaking his head. "I just couldn't lose you. Please, Stevie… please… just tell me what I did to hurt you. Whatever it is, I'll undo it somehow."

"You didn't do anything," Stevie said, her voice still soft. "You were devastated when Dave asked Susan to marry him… and… I just couldn't take being second best."

"Second best?" he echoed, his face indicating shock. "Jesus, Stevie." He shook his head. "You're talking about that night when you found me at the bar?" Stevie nodded. "I was drunk," he said, his expression indicating that she should have known that.

189

"I know. You were drunk, and when I tried to help you, you pulled away from me… and I saw it in your eyes, the desolation. And it hurt. It physically hurt," she said, tears coming to her eyes.

"Stevie," he said, trailing off as he touched her cheek. "God, I was drunk and feeling bereft. Not because I had lost Susan, but because I figured I was never going to find what she just had. You and I were so damned busy keeping it casual, I just… God, Stevie." He shook his head again, turning away. The muscles in his jaw twitched as he clenched his teeth. He looked back at her, seeing right into her soul. "I love you, okay? I love you. I couldn't admit to myself that I loved you, because I couldn't get over the idea that I was supposed to be in love with Susan. But then you were so mad at me, and pushed me so far away, and the shit with that other guy, and your venom… But I just kept coming back for more, because I couldn't leave it alone." He sighed deeply. "I couldn't leave you alone."

Stevie stared back at him. When he stopped, she didn't speak for a long minute. Finally she grinned. "It's about fucking time, Collins."

"What?" he said, stunned.

"It's about damned time you decided you love me. And I have news for you, pal—you're not the only one."

"Not the only one, what?" Christian asked, giving her a suspicious look.

Stevie grinned. "The only one in love, you idiot."

"You?" he asked, too surprised to say more.

"Well, duh. Why do you think I was so mad at you?"

"Because you thought I was still in love with Susan."

"And using me as a Band-Aid."

Christian shook his head. "After San Francisco, I thought we got through all that shit."

"We did, and then you went back and negated it with your comment about honesty being a problem too."

"Only after you turned into the ice queen from hell."

"So I thought I understood, okay?"

"I don't suppose it occurs to you, O'Neil, to bloody ask, does it?"

"Well, no," Stevie said, starting to grin impishly.

He leaned forward, his face only an inch from hers. "You're gonna be the death of me, I can just tell."

"Only if you're lucky," she replied, and kissed him.

CHAPTER 6

Six months later the headline in the *San Diego Tribune* read:

Drug Kingpin Goes Down

Marco Tiempo was convicted today on ten counts of drug trafficking, two counts of attempted murder of a peace officer—Sergeant Rhiannon Templeton and Sergeant Stevie O'Neil—and one count of murder of a peace officer, Sergeant Jason Templeton, while evading arrest. Tiempo was sentenced to life in prison without the possibility of parole. Templeton's widow, Sergeant Rhiannon Templeton, stated, "I'm glad that Mr. Tiempo has finally received punishment for the murder of my husband. Who knows how many other lives he's ruined with his blatant disregard for human life. I'm very happy with the verdict." Mrs. Templeton's sister, Sergeant Stevie O'Neil, had one comment about Marco Tiempo: "The bastard got what he deserved, only not soon enough to save my brother-in-law's life."

Ms. O'Neil was a key witness in the case against Tiempo, having been his bodyguard while acting in an undercover capacity for the San Diego Police Department. The case had been postponed due to the attempted murder of Ms. O'Neil by people acting on

```
orders of the defendant. Ms. O'Neil was
struck three times by high-speed rifle
rounds, but fortunately doctors were able
to save her life. San Diego Police Depart-
ment has yet another hard-won victory un-
der its belt, and the message to drug deal-
ers is "Stay out, or we'll take you down,"
as stated by Chief Midnight Chevalier-De-
benshire.
```

"Come on, O'Neil, we're gonna hit traffic," Christian said, leaning out the window of the Viper.

"Bite me, Collins," Stevie said, coming out of the apartment clipping her badge to her belt. She got in the car and saw that he was grinning at her.

"Don't give me that grin," she said, smiling. "You made us late this morning." He had made them late, finding it absolutely necessary to make love to her in bed, and then again in the shower.

"I didn't hear any complaints then," he replied, putting the car into gear and backing out.

"And you won't, but you'll get your ass kicked if you hassle me about making us hit traffic," she said, reaching over to smack him on the arm.

Christian laughed as he headed down the road. Stevie was working out at the task force now, having completed a short training "course" with Dave and another narcotics identification course at the same time. It had been a grueling six months, between that and rehabilitation. She'd had Christian there to push her, though, doing his own rehabilitation on his shoulder at the same time. The bullet that

193

had hit him had shattered his shoulder, and it had taken three surgeries before they felt he was repaired enough to start rehab. Even then it had been a painful process.

Stevie had been labeled the department's own "moving target" for having sustained three hits and still lived. It had earned her a reputation of being unstoppable—not that she'd had anything to do with surviving other than luck, at least as far as she was concerned. Christian, on the other hand, was convinced that she'd fought for her life so she could make his miserable. At least, that's what he told her often enough when they were in rehab and she was yelling at him to do one more rep. In truth, he'd found that being with Stevie on a full-time basis was indeed exciting and kept him on his toes all the time. Although they weren't officially living together, he spent more nights at her apartment than he did at Joe's. And when he was at Joe's because Joe went out of town, Stevie stayed with him most of those nights.

There were a number of times when he was sure he was going to kill her, because she never took any of the crap he dished out. If she thought he was being one way about something, she'd do the exact opposite of what he'd said should be done. They had seriously intense fights, but even better intense love-making to make up for it.

As he dropped her off at the task force, she kissed him. The kiss deepened immediately as their bodies remembered the love-making from earlier that morning.

"Hey, you two, not in the parking lot, okay?" Bob Forrester said, grinning at them.

Stevie laughed as she looked up at her new boss, and Christian leaned his head out the window.

"Hey, Blue," Bob said, nodding to him.

"Hey, Forrester," Christian said, nodding back to the other man.

Stevie got out of the car. She looked good, wearing black jeans, low-heeled boots, and a black tank top with a burgundy suede jacket. Both Christian and Forrester admired her as she walked around the Viper to the driver's side.

"Looking good, O'Neil," Bob said, holding back a grin. He always enjoyed baiting Christian.

Christian grabbed Stevie's hand and pulled her down to kiss her deeply, his hand on her cheek. She kissed him back with equal passion. When their lips parted, Christian looked at Forrester. "So long as you remember who she belongs to." He grinned then, gunning the engine of the Viper, and drove off. Stevie watched him go with a smile on her face.

***

In his office, Rick picked up the phone. It was the call he'd been waiting for for days. Thank God, it was ready! He made some arrangements then hung up, grinning with satisfaction. Joe walked in at that point.

"What did I miss?" he asked, moving to sit down in front of Rick's desk.

"I got it."

"You did?" Joe asked, his grin starting.

"Yup."

"When will it be here?"

"In time for Christmas."

"Too right," Joe said, high-fiving Rick.

***

Kyle woke next to Rhiannon, knowing he needed to get up but not wanting to leave the warmth of their bed. She'd moved in with him the month before. Brenden was thoroughly enjoying having a woman around. Nick, who at first had been angry that his father was moving another woman into their lives, was slowly but surely coming around. Rhiannon stirred and turned over, opening her eyes and looking up into his.

He kissed her deeply.

"Good morning to you too," Rhiannon said, smiling warmly.

Kyle snuggled down next to her again, kissing her shoulder. "See, you have to admit this is much better than having to get up and run home to take a shower and get ready for work."

"Yes, dear," Rhiannon said, shaking her head. "And I've admitted that every day for a month. Are you proud of yourself yet?"

Kyle laughed. "Not quite yet."

"What's on your agenda for today?"

"Meetings, meetings, and… oh yeah, meetings."

"Oh, sounds like fun," Rhiannon said, making a face.

"Oh, Joe wanted to find out if we're going there for Christmas."

Rhiannon shrugged. "If you want to. It's up to you. I don't know how you want to do it with the boys and all."

"Well, I think we could head over there after we do Christmas morning here."

"Sounds like a good idea," she said, glad that she was looking forward to Christmas again.

Being with Kyle had brought her back to life. She smiled all the time now, her green eyes always alight with warmth. Now when she thought of Jason, it was with a deep affection, but not with the searing heartache it used to cause. Kyle had given the picture of Barbara that he'd kept by his bedside to Brenden, who now kept it by his bedside. Rhiannon had told Kyle that the picture didn't bother her, but Kyle had said that he thought it was something he should do out of respect for his relationship with her.

Rhiannon had made a point of taking the 5 x 7 photo of Barbara to the photo shop and had had it blown up into an 8 x 10. She had a special frame made for it, and planned to give it to Kyle and the boys for Christmas. She had no intention of attempting to replace Barbara in their lives, only to share their lives with them.

Rhiannon didn't know that Kyle had taken Jason's badge and had a custom shadow box frame made for it, and was planning to give that to her for Christmas. It was their way of showing respect for the other's love for the one they had lost.

***

Donovan woke up feeling refreshed after having slept for fourteen hours. He'd just gotten back from his undercover stint. He rolled over and dialed Erin's desk. She picked up on the third ring.

"You free for lunch?" he asked.

"Maybe," she said, grinning to herself.

"What do I have to do?" he asked. "Beg?"

"Never. What time will you be here?"

"Noon."

"I'll be ready," she said, hanging up with a smile. She looked up as Christian walked in. "You're late, Mr. Collins."

"Yeah, well…" he said, grinning evilly. "You know how it is…"

"Yeah," Erin countered. "Terrible, being in love and all, huh?"

"Takes a lot of energy. And stamina."

"Oh God!" Erin said, making a horrified face, then laughed. "That was TMI, Mr. Collins."

Christian laughed, not looking sorry in the slightest.

At noon, Donovan walked into the office to pick Erin up.

"Hey, Blue," he said.

"Hey, Donovan."

"You ready?" Donovan asked Erin.

"Yep," she said, standing up.

"You kids be good," Christian said with a leering grin.

"Shut up!" Erin said, careful to slap him on the good shoulder.

Christian laughed. "I know, I know—you're just friends, right?"

"Right," Donovan said, grinning.

"Bullshit," Christian said, under his breath but loud enough for Donovan to hear.

Erin and he walked out to his car. He opened the door for her and she got in. They had lunch at a nearby restaurant, and on the way back he stopped by the bay and they sat and talked for a while.

"So when does Bobby get out for Christmas break?" Donovan asked, leaning against the hood of the Mustang, watching as she balanced on the heavy beam that separated the parking lot from the sidewalk.

"The end of this week."

Donovan nodded. "And you're coming to Joe's, right?"

"I think so, if you're sure it's okay," she said, sounding unsure of herself.

"Erin, I told you, Joe told me to invite you personally."

Erin looked up at him, smiling. It was so nice to have people that worried about her. She remembered well how the situation with Tyler had been resolved three months before.

Donovan had gotten tired of the waiting game and had told Erin's old roommates to give Tyler his number when he called again, which he did frequently. Tyler called Donovan's house, and Donovan answered.

"Who's this?" Tyler asked belligerently.

"Donovan. Who's this?" Donovan said, although he was fairly sure he knew.

"Tyler Bodine. You the guy Erin's shacking up with?"

"That would be me, yeah."

"I'm gonna kick your ass, man. I'm gonna fuck you up bad. You're sleeping with a married woman—did you know that?"

"Yeah, I know."

"You motherfucker, I'm gonna kick your fucking ass."

"Why don't we meet and discuss this, Mr. Bodine."

"Meet, my ass—I'm gonna fuck you up."

"Do you know where the Mission Beach roller coaster is?"

"Yeah, I know where it is."

"Meet me there at three tomorrow," Donovan said, and hung up.

The following day, Tyler arrived feeling very full of himself. He was pumped up on alcohol and a few uppers. He was going to kick this guy's ass and show Erin not to screw around. He was going to fuck her, then beat her down for leaving him. As he walked up to the parking lot for the Mission Beach roller coaster, he started noticing people there. There was an old Dodge Charger with a dude leaning against it, with a nasty-looking gun in his hand down at his side. There was a blue Viper with a dark-haired guy leaning against the hood, next to a really hot-looking redhead. The man wore a shoulder holster with a gun in it; the chick had a gun on her hip. There was a badass green Mustang with two long-haired dudes resting against the hood, both wearing nasty-looking guns too. A hot blond leaned against a white car, her arms crossed, and she held a gun as well. There was a big guy standing next to an Explorer, another redhead beside him and an Asian guy in front of the car, and a big Samoan woman next to an old Camaro. Who the fuck were these people? And where was this Donovan?

Then he saw him, leaning against the driver's door of a new-model black Mustang. His arms were crossed over his chest, his legs crossed at the ankles. Tyler started to walk toward him. As he passed

200

the other people, they fell in behind him. Tyler was getting pretty nervous by the time he got to Donovan. He saw Erin sitting in the passenger seat of the Mustang.

"You Tyler Bodine?" Donovan asked, unnecessarily.

"Y-y-yeah," Tyler said, not feeling so brave anymore. "Y-y-you need all these people to face me?" he asked with false bravado.

Donovan's eyes flicked to the people standing behind Tyler, then back to him. "No, I don't need them. I can kick your ass all on my own."

"Then t-t-try it."

"Well," said a voice from behind him. Tyler looked back at the tall man with dirty-blond hair. "That's the thing."

"He doesn't need us," Rick said.

"But we're his family," Dave said.

"And family sticks together," Spider put in.

"And we don't like anyone fucking with our family," Kana said.

"And you threatening Erin is fucking with our family," Tiny said.

"So we see you as a problem," Christian said.

"And we don't like problems," Stevie said.

"No, we don't," Jess said.

"So, Mr. Bodine," Midnight said, moving through the group as they parted for her. "You'd better get your ass back to wherever you came from, or you're going to find out what happens to people that we don't like."

Tyler looked back at Midnight for a long minute, his face taking

201

on a leer.

"I wouldn't do it if I were you," Joe warned.

Rick grinned. "Oh, let him do it."

"Boys..." Midnight said.

"Woman like you needs a man, right?" Tyler said.

Midnight had time to shake her head and step out of the way before Rick's fist knocked him to the ground. She stood looking down at Tyler. "No, I have a man, thanks." Rick stood behind her, leaning down to kiss her neck.

Tyler left town that day and hadn't been heard from since.

Thinking about what Donovan had done for her, Erin hopped down off the beam and walked over to him, putting her arms around his neck and leaning against him. She looked up at him and then got up on her tiptoes to kiss his lips.

"What was that for?" he asked, grinning.

"Lunch," she said, kissing him again.

"And that?"

"For picking me up," she said with another kiss.

"And that?"

"For calling me this morning." After a while they stopped talking and just kissed for a long time. Eventually he took her back to the department. On his way out he ran into Jeanie coming in.

"Hey, Jay," he said, smiling. "How's it going?"

She grinned. "It's going. What are you doing here?"

"Lunch with Erin."

"Ah," she said, nodding. "We still on for dinner?"

"Yep, I'm making your favorite."

"Pepper steak?"

"Yes, ma'am," he said, smiling.

"Cool."

"Be there at seven."

"Which means dinner will be ready at eight," she said, wagging her finger at him.

"You're always late."

"And you love it."

He grinned. "Oh yeah, it's the anticipation."

"Brat!" she said, swatting him on the arm.

Donovan laughed, and kissed her on the cheek. "See you at seven."

"I'll be on time!" she said as he walked away.

"Yeah, sure, right."

She was a half hour late that night.

He opened the door grinning and looking at his watch.

"Hey, I was a half hour better than you thought," she said, walking in.

"Uh-huh," Donovan said, heading back into the kitchen.

Jeanie sat on the low island, admiring him. He wore beige khakis, a black shirt, and black boots.

"You look good, Curtis," she said, reaching behind her and taking a wine glass down from the rack.

Donovan walked over with the wine bottle, pouring for her as he looked down at her. "You think so?"

"Yep," she said, smiling up at him.

He leaned down and kissed her on the lips. "Thanks." He turned back to the stove.

They had dinner and talked about all the things she was doing on patrol. She'd told Joe about her problem with her Field Training Officer on the first go-around, and Joe had made sure that she got a younger, less chauvinistic FTO this time. She was much happier now.

Frank Dominguez had called her a few times, but she'd put him off. She'd gone back to San Francisco long enough to pack her clothes and things and put in her resignation. She'd been back on the force in San Diego for five months. She was still working on earning Donovan's trust and love back, and she knew full well that he was seeing Erin too.

They'd discussed it one night, and he'd told her that he didn't think he wanted to get into a big, serious relationship again for a while, that he cared about both her and Erin, but that he didn't want to make any commitments anymore. Jeanie knew it was her fault he was gun-shy now, so she knew she had no right to bitch about what he wanted. So she worked with what she could get. Jeanie knew what she wanted, because she knew what she'd had with Donovan before, and she wanted it back. No matter how long it took her, or until that terrible day when he told her he was in love with someone else.

That night after dinner they ended up making love. It was great—it was always great. He just didn't snuggle up next to her, telling her how much he loved her, anymore. She missed that, but she knew she'd blown that too. One day, she told herself, one day he'd say it again.

***

Dave walked out of the ocean, dropping his board on the sand and lying down next to Susan. She came with him almost every morning when he surfed, sitting on the beach and watching him. Afterward they'd talk, or just watch the sky light up as the sun rose behind them. Dave's undercover cases took him away from her for two to three days a week, but then he'd be back, waking her up in the middle of the night. Kissing her for hours, holding her, making love to her. Joe would always know when Dave was back in town; Susan would look exhausted when she got there to pick the kids up for school. His favorite phrase was "The man with the cross is back." Randy would swat him on the butt and tell him to stop teasing Susan.

Susan had set to work decorating Dave's home, which he reminded her constantly was their home. Living with another person had taken an adjustment for Dave, since he hadn't done it since he was about seventeen. Susan was patient and quiet about his little habits that drove her crazy. The habit of drinking right out of the milk carton was stopped quickly, however.

Dave would come home from being undercover to find that his house had been changed just a little bit more. She had, however, left his living room as he liked it, only adding some pictures. And she'd been careful about the ones she'd selected. She'd been particularly excited to show him the room when he'd come home from a case three months after they were married. She'd been nervous, but excited at the same time.

When he'd arrived, she'd shown him the oak-framed pictures she'd bought. They showed lighthouses with stormy seas, and there was one of an old clipper ship going down in rough water. Dave had stood and stared for so long that Susan was crestfallen, thinking he didn't like them. When he turned to her, he said, "I love them. Thank you, honey." He had kissed her deeply then, picking her up and carrying her over to the couch, eventually making love to her there. Afterward, he lay holding her, looking at the pictures again. He'd told her about loving ships as a kid, and always loving to be near the ocean during a storm.

"Are we going to Joe's for Christmas?" Susan asked him as they lay on the sand.

Dave leaned back, catching the first morning rays on his face and closing his eyes. "Christmas is when?"

Susan smiled down at him. He was always forgetting dates and days because of the way his work kept him. "Christmas is on Thursday, love."

"Yeah, I should be back by then."

"Back?" Susan asked, worried. He'd only been home a day and a half.

"Yeah, I got a short one this week."

"David…" Susan said, concerned that he was overdoing it.

"I'm okay, babe," he said, reaching up to touch her shoulder. "I'll rest over Christmas, I promise."

"You'd better," she said, knowing that she'd have to practically sit on him to keep him from doing too much.

"So," he said, sitting up and looking at her. "What do you want for Christmas?"

"You, home safe."

He grinned, kissing her. "That's not considered an answer, Mrs. Dibbins."

"Well, it will have to do, Mr. Dibbins."

"Fine, I'll just have to find something on my own..."

"Oh no you don't!" she said. "The last time I let you do something on your own you almost cleaned out your savings." She held up her hand and wiggled the beautiful wedding set he'd bought her.

"You were worth every penny," he said, smiling warmly.

She smiled back. "Well, I want a card for Christmas."

"You got it, babe."

He had every intention of giving her a card. Of course, inside the card were two round-trip tickets to London so she could see her family. But he didn't figure he'd tell her that at this point. Let her kill him later.

Susan looked down at him. She was sure he was plotting something but didn't have the heart to harass him about it. He so enjoyed giving her things. His gifts were always thoughtful and sweet; he often brought her flowers home too. He told her he'd missed that for the past so many years, being so old when he got married, so he had a lot to make up for.

She was still hoping she'd made the right decision for him for Christmas. She'd bought him the custom wheels he'd been eyeing for the Charger. He'd dismissed the idea of buying them since they were $600 each. But Susan had bought them and was hoping he hadn't changed his mind about wanting them. She had no idea that Dave still looked at them every day when he went by the shop where they were displayed. But with a wife and a home to look after, he just couldn't justify spending almost $2,500 on wheels. He just day-dreamed about them constantly.

***

Stevie and Christian were staying at Joe's house on Christmas Eve, so they could be there at a decent hour in the morning. Christian was helping Joe put JT's and Kat's new bikes together. Stevie and Randy sat watching them, murmuring to each other. It was entertaining to see the men try to figure out where everything went, especially after they started drinking shots every time they got a part put on, to toast their good luck.

"You realize we're going to get stuck putting those things to-gether, right?" Stevie said in a low whisper.

Randy laughed. "You mean after they pass out?"

Stevie chuckled. "Yep."

Randy sighed and sat back against the sofa. "You know anything about putting bikes together?"

"Nope," Stevie said, shaking her head and grinning.

"I'll go get another bottle of tequila," Randy said, standing up as Stevie laughed.

It had been a fun evening.

Stevie woke the next morning to the sound of kids' shouts of glee. She looked over at Christian, sleeping next to her. He was lying on his side, facing her, his arm around her waist. She was still constantly amazed at how handsome he was. Carefully, she moved out from under his arm and went to her overnight bag to pull out his Christmas present. She wanted to give it to him privately, afraid he wouldn't like it and knowing he wouldn't be honest with her in front of a group.

"Steve?" he said drowsily, reaching for where she'd been lying.

"I'm here, babe," she said, sitting back down on the bed.

He pulled her down to kiss her. "What are you doing up so early?"

"It's Christmas morning, babe. The kids got up a half hour ago."

Christian lay back against the pillows, not looking ready to get up yet. "What's that?" he asked, pointing to the box she held.

"Your Christmas present," she said, and handed it to him.

"You don't want to wait?"

"No, I want you to open it now," she said, looking nervous.

He grinned, sitting up. Stevie's eyes were drawn to his chest. "God, you are gorgeous," she said, leaning over to kiss his chest. She felt his rumble of laughter under her lips.

"You get me started this morning, and we're never going to get out there."

"Good point," she said, moving back and looking at him. "Open it," she said, gesturing to the box in his hand.

He laughed. "Okay, okay. Worse than the kids, I tell ya," he was saying as he pulled the ribbon and wrapping paper off. He opened the small box and Stevie held her breath. Christian lifted the bracelet out and set the box down, examining the intricately carved but heavy gold links.

"It's called a Maserati style," Stevie said, biting her lip, trying to decide if he liked it or not.

Christian looked up at her, smiling. "It's fantastic."

"You like it?"

"I love it, and you," he said, leaning over and kissing her deeply. Then he handed her the bracelet and held out his left wrist. "Put it on me, will ya?"

Stevie fastened the bracelet around his wrist. It did look really good on him. The gold glowed against his dark skin.

"I've seen you wear a bracelet before, I just didn't know…"

"This one is better than that one," he said. "I won't take this one off."

Stevie kissed him. "I'm glad you like it, babe."

"Well," he said, leaning back and opening the bedside drawer, "since you gave me my Christmas present, I guess I'll have to give you yours now too." With that he dropped a small square velvet box in her hand. A ring box. Stevie gave him a wary look and he laughed, shaking his head. "No, babe, I'm not that stupid." He knew neither of them was ready for that.

Stevie opened the box. Nestled inside the black velvet was an emerald-and-diamond ring. The emerald was square-cut with two diamond baguettes on either side. The whole thing was surrounded by round diamonds.

"Oh my God, Christian…" she said, speechless.

Christian smiled, taking the box from her and taking the ring out. He picked up her left hand, placing it on her ring finger. She looked at him questioningly; he'd just put it on the traditional wedding finger.

He grinned. "I figure possession is nine-tenths of the law, right?"

"Right..." Stevie said, mystified.

"Well," he said, leaning in to kiss her, "I'm the other tenth."

He took the time to remind her of how much he craved her, and to make her crave him as well. Afterward they lay together, catching their breath. She propped herself up on her elbow, looking down at him as he lay on his back.

"Christian?" she said, reaching out to touch his chest.

"Yeah?"

"Is this different?"

"Different?" he asked, confused. Then understanding dawned. "You mean different from Susan?"

"Yeah..."

"Of course it is, Steve. You're about as different from Susan as night is from day."

"Yeah, but, I mean... you said that after six months of being with her only, you got to where you wanted to start screwing around. Is it that way for you now?"

Christian turned on his side, sliding his hand up the side of her body. "No, Steve, it's not."

"You'd tell me the truth, right?"

He looked at her for a long moment, then leaned forward to kiss her. "Yes, I'd tell you. I told Susan, right?"

"True."

"I want to be with you," he assured her. "No one does for me what you do." He kissed her lips again, moving her to her back and lying half over her, looking down into her eyes. "What would you say to us getting a place together?"

"You mean officially living together?"

"Well, hell, we spend just about every night together anyway," he said, grinning. "And God knows I can't sleep for shit when you're not here, so... yeah, officially living together."

Stevie knew this was a huge commitment for Christian, and she found herself grinning over the fact that she'd actually gotten that much out of him. She pulled him down, kissing him and running her hands over his back.

"I'm hoping that means you like the idea," he murmured against her lips.

"Oh yeah, living with you should be interesting," she said, smiling.

"Okay, you're really pushing it now, O'Neil."

"I love the idea, Christian," she said, kissing him again. The made love again, enjoying each other thoroughly. They didn't emerge from the bedroom for another two hours, both looking sated and happy.

"Good morning," Joe said, his grin wry.

"Morning," Christian said, moving to sit down on the couch. Stevie came in a couple of minutes later carrying a mug of coffee.

"Morning," she murmured as she sat down next to Christian, turning to put her back against his side as he wrapped his arm around her. She sipped the coffee then handed it to him. The kids excitedly showed them all of their new toys, then got busy playing.

"We'll do the adult stuff later, when everyone gets here," Joe said with a grin.

"We cheated," Christian said, holding up his left wrist.

Randy looked at Stevie. "He liked it?"

"Yep," Stevie said, grinning. "I got rewarded for it too." She held out her hand.

Randy looked at the ring Christian had given her, askance at the placement.

"No, it's not an engagement ring," Stevie said, laughing.

"It's a ring of possession," Christian put in, smiling.

They spent the next couple of hours getting showers and cleaning up the kids' debris from their gift-opening. Rick and Midnight got there at two that afternoon with Mikeyla and Ricardo. Ricardo went off to play with JT and Kat. Mikeyla asked Randy if she could use the computer. Randy nodded, and Mikeyla disappeared down the hall.

Kyle and Rhiannon were next to arrive, with Nick and Brenden. Brenden asked where JT was; Joe pointed in the direction of the kids' rooms. He ran off, hauling his newest truck to show JT. Nick stood looking uncomfortably around all the adults.

"The computer is down the hall," Joe said. Nick nodded and walked in that direction. Everyone laughed.

Donovan, Jeanie, and Erin showed up at the same time Dave and Susan got there. Erin's son, Bobby, ran off to find the other children.

Tiny and Jess turned up an hour later with Spider and Tammy right behind them. Kana arrived last.

They sat around drinking various wines, beers, and shots. Then they started opening presents. Dave and Susan exchanged first. She had to have Joe help her bring the box to Dave. It was only one of the wheels; the rest they'd already snuck into Dave's trunk. Dave looked at the box, and then at Susan.

"Open it!" she said, laughing.

He unwrapped the package, then lifted the lid off the box. He sat back and just stared openmouthed. Then he started to grin, and everyone laughed.

"You still wanted them, didn't you?" Susan asked, worried.

"Oh yeah…" Dave said, still staring at the wheel.

"Someone get Dave a drink," Joe said.

"Or a cold shower," Rick put in, and everyone laughed again. They all knew the way Dave could get about car stuff.

Dave chuckled and kissed Susan. "Thank you."

"The other three are in your trunk," she said.

"Oh, I get all four?"

"Scamp!" she said, swatting him on the arm.

He laughed, then reached into his jacket pocket and took out the card for her, looking humbled. "I'm sorry," he said as he handed her the envelope. "You said you only wanted a card."

"Yes, I did," Susan said, smiling at him. She opened the card, and out fell the airline tickets into her lap. She stared down at them, then gave Dave a narrowed look. "You scoundrel," she said, picking the tickets up and reading the destination. "London?" she breathed, smiling as tears came to her eyes. He knew she'd been missing her home for a while and wanting to see her friends and family again.

Dave grinned, happy to see that she was pleased. She kissed him, thanking him sincerely.

Kyle and Rhiannon exchanged next. Kyle opened the box for him and the boys, with Nick and Brenden looking on from behind the couch. Kyle stared in awe at the framed photograph of Barbara. He looked up at Rhiannon, his eyes saying everything that wouldn't come out of his mouth because of the lump in his throat. He hugged her tight. "Thank you," he whispered.

"I want it on the fireplace," she whispered back.

He leaned back then and handed her her gift. She opened it and lifted the shadow box out of the tissue paper. Tears slid down her cheeks as she saw Jason's badge nestled inside. She hugged Kyle, unable to speak.

"Oh, there's one more thing," he said, moving off the couch to get down on one knee. Everyone in the room held their breath.

Kyle pulled out a small velvet box and opened it. Inside was an engagement ring, a marquise-cut diamond set in brushed gold with diamond baguettes in the band.

"Rhiannon, will you marry me?" Kyle asked, taking her hand.

"Marry us," Brenden put in, making everyone laugh.

Kyle grinned at his son, then glanced at Nick, who nodded slowly. "Will you marry us?"

Rhiannon smiled brilliantly, nodding as she moved to hug Kyle.

"That's a yes, right?" Rick asked, and got a smack on the head from Midnight.

"Looked like a yes to me," Dave put in.

"I'd second that," Joe said, grinning.

Rhiannon laughed. "It's a yes," she said, looking up at Kyle.

"Thank God," Spider said, his usual sentiment for these occasions.

Kyle laughed as he put the ring on her finger, then kissed her softly. Everyone clapped.

Spider and Tammy had already exchanged gifts at home, and so had Donovan and the girls, so it was up to Rick and Midnight to go next. Midnight handed Rick his present. It was a shoe-sized box. He took it and noticed it was extremely light. When he shook it there was no sound.

"Great, I get an empty box," he said, grinning.

"Shut up, Debenshire, or you'll get a bruised shin too," Midnight said, smiling sweetly.

Rick unwrapped the box and lifted the lid off, then stared at the contents in confusion. He reached in and picked up a yellow card, which looked like one of the cards they used to request leave. And indeed, upon inspection, it was.

"Okay, I'm officially confused," he said, grinning.

"Read the card, Debenshire," Midnight said, rolling her eyes.

He read his name, his unit, and the date of the card, being Christmas day. The box for vacation was checked, and the dates listed were December 26 through January 8. It was signed by Kyle Masterson as approved.

He looked at Midnight, still bewildered. "You're ordering me to take time off?"

Midnight breathed a deep sigh. "Look under the tissue paper, Richard."

Rick dug to the bottom of the box and found two airline tickets. He read the destination: Tahiti. His eyes grew wide as he looked back at the dates on the tickets.

"Is this what I think it is?" he said, not daring to hope.

"It's called a vacation, babe. Just me and you, for two weeks in Tahiti, no kids, no cops, no phones, no faxes, no meetings."

He grinned. "No shooting?"

Midnight laughed. "Let's hope not."

"Oh, babe..." he said, shaking his head and pulling her into his arms. "I love you. Thank you. I need this with you."

"I know you do," Midnight said. "We both do."

He kissed her, hugging her tight. He'd been begging her to take a vacation with just him for two years. Finally he was getting his wish.

"Now for your present," he said, and handed her a small rectangular box.

Midnight shook it, then opened it. She picked up a shiny new key, and then looked at him. "Key to your heart?"

"You had that a long time ago, babe. Turn it over."

Midnight turned the key over and noted the Chevy symbol on it. She narrowed her eyes at him. "Richard, I told you I didn't want a new one," she said, thinking he had been crazy enough to buy her a new Corvette. He had begged her to let him replace her 'Vette with a new one, but she had refused, stating that she wanted her old one back.

"Just go look outside," Rick said, his smile warm.

Midnight got up and walked to Joe's front door. Rick followed, as did the rest of the group. When Midnight opened the door, her heart stopped. It was her car—she was sure of it. She stood in the doorway, her mouth hanging open.

"But how…"

"It's not your original, babe, but it's the same year, same everything inside. I even added the CD player back, and as many of your disks as I could find to replace the ones you lost," Rick said. He winked. "This one even has fewer miles on it."

Midnight walked down the steps and slid her hand over the fender of the car. He was right—it wasn't hers. The dent she'd put in it with her boot heel years ago wasn't there. She walked around the car, then got into it. It smelled the same. The same leather everything.

"Rick… Rick…" she said, shaking her head. He stood watching her gape and enjoyed every moment of it. He'd been working on the project for just under a year now. He'd finally found the right car to replace her beloved Corvette.

Midnight jumped out of the car and hugged him tight. He lifted her off her feet, kissing her deeply.

"I love you. Thank you so much, babe," she said, smiling, her gold-green eyes shining up at him. She couldn't express in words how much his gift meant to her.

After a long while everyone went back into the house. It was Joe and Randy's turn to exchange. Joe said he wanted to go first, so Randy let him. He reached into his pocket, pulled out a set of keys, and placed them in her hand.

She grinned. "A new car?"

"Nope."

"My own house, because you're tired of living with me?"

"Close, actually."

Randy smiled. "Explain."

"It's the keys to a house," he said, "but not to live in." He touched her under the chin. "It's for your center. I bought the building."

"Joe…" Randy said, unable to believe what he'd just said. "You bought an entire building for me?"

"Well, it's not really a building per se," he said, grinning as he handed her a large manila envelope.

Randy opened the envelope and took out an 11 x 14 glossy of the biggest, most beautiful Victorian house she'd ever seen.

"This?" she asked, stunned.

"That," he said, smiling. "It's in Old Town, so it's generally centrally located, and it's already set up as a boarding-type house, so you won't have to do a lot. It's got all the original wood and fixtures, so it's already got a homey feel to it…" He trailed off as Randy threw herself into his arms. He laughed, and she kissed him over and over again.

"Thank you, thank you, thank you," she said, over and over. "I love it—I love you. God, you are crazy! But I love you."

It took a long time for her to calm down enough to give him his present; she couldn't believe what he had done. Finally, taking a deep breath and blowing it out, she got up and left the room, coming back a minute later with a big box; it was obviously heavy. Dave jumped up and took it from her hands, setting it down in front of Joe.

"Thanks, Dave," Randy said, smiling at him. He nodded as he sat back down next to Susan.

Joe leaned forward, testing the weight of the box. "Jesus!" he said, grinning. "It's weights, and you're telling me I'm getting fat."

"Joe, there isn't an ounce of fat on you," Randy said.

"Except in his head," Rick put in.

"Don't make me shoot you in my own house," Joe said, laughing with everyone else.

Joe ripped off the paper and got to the filament tape the box had been secured with. He pulled out the Spyderco knife he always carried and flipped it open. He cut the tape and lifted the lid off the box, then started pulling aside the tissue paper. There were a number of navy blue leather-bound volumes with years printed in antique gold on each spine. He lifted out the volume with the earliest year, and when he opened it he was stunned to see his mother's handwriting.

"Oh my God..." he said, trailing off as he scanned the words on the inside of the front cover. *For my son, Joseph Michael Sinclair. Lovingly kept to remind you of how much we will love you in the years to come. Live a long and happy life, my son. ~ Cynthia Sinclair*

There was no describing how it felt to read those words. Joe felt as if his heart had stopped. He looked through the pages; each had a date. His mother had kept a journal from the day she had found out she was carrying a child.

"My God, Randy," he said, looking at her with tears in his eyes. "How did you find this?"

Randy smiled. "Sandra Bender found the journals in the attic.

Apparently your mother had been storing them up there. When Sandra went through them she found that the last year was missing, so she went down to your parents' room and found it. Joe, she wrote in it the morning before she died."

Joe shook his head, unable to believe the gift Randy had bestowed on him. She had given him back his mother. There were no words to describe how he felt. Tears flowed from his eyes as he hugged her tight. "I love you, so much," he whispered.

Sandra Bender had called Randy four months before, having unearthed the books, and Randy had asked her to overnight them as soon as possible. She had spent the next four months having pages in the older books restored and then having the books rebound, since the original bindings were literally falling apart. She had known what it would mean to Joe to be able to read his mother's words and thoughts. And the inscription his mother had put into each book was something that Randy herself couldn't have written better if she'd tried. It had taken every speck of control she'd had to keep the books from Joe until Christmas, but she'd known it would be a perfect gift for him.

Everyone in the room was quiet. Midnight had tears in her eyes, as did Rick. It was a perfect end to the exchange of gifts.

It took Joe quite a while to get over the effects of seeing his mother's handwriting. He was dying to shut himself away and just read her words.

They had dinner an hour later, sitting around the table, talking and laughing happily as a group. Joe looked around at all of his friends, and he smiled. The family was indeed growing, and he liked it. He lifted his glass up in a toast.

"To life, love, and the pursuit of happiness."

"Amen," Rick said.

"We're not toasting to FORS anymore?" Dave asked.

"No one's in FORS anymore," Tiny countered.

"Excuse me?" Rick said, grinning.

"Oh yeah, except Debenshire."

"Oh yeah, except Debenshire," Rick echoed, giving Tiny a dirty look.

"Children," Midnight said, grinning.

"What?" Rick and Tiny said together, both looking innocent.

Midnight glanced at Joe. He rolled his eyes and shook his head. "Don't make me send you to your rooms," Midnight said.

Rick grinned. "Only if you go with me."

"Hey now, none of that at the dinner table," Christian put in.

"Hear, hear," Susan said, winking at him.

"Yeah, there are children present," Dave said.

"Just because you married her…" Spider said, starting to grin.

"Oh, low blow, Spider," Dave said, but he was grinning too.

"I am not a child!" Susan exclaimed.

"No, she's not…" Christian said, his tone leering.

"Watch it, Collins," Dave said, throwing him a dirty look.

Christian stuck his tongue out at Dave, who stunned everyone by doing the same.

"Oh, Jesus," Stevie said, laughing at them. "Susan, you take yours, I'll take mine."

Susan laughed and grabbed Dave, kissing him. Stevie did the same to Christian, leaving both men grinning.

"You know, could we just have a simple toast here?" Joe asked, shaking his head like a disappointed father.

"Then do the right damned toast," Kana said.

"Fine," Joe said, sighing. "To FORS."

"To FORS!"

You can find more information about the author and series here:

www.sherrylhancock.com

www.facebook.com/SherrylDHancock

www.vulpine-press.com/midknight-blue-series

Also by Sherryl D. Hancock:

The *WeHo* series follows a group of women from Los Angeles as they navigate the ups and downs of love, life, work, and everything in between.

www.vulpine-press.com/we-ho

The *Wild Irish Silence* series. Escape into the world of BJ Sparks and discover how he went from the small-town boy to the world-famous rock star.

www.vulpine-press.com/wild-irish-silence-series

www.ingramcontent.com/pod-product-compliance
Lightning Source LLC
Chambersburg PA
CBHW031729170626
46808CB00005B/1939

* 9 7 8 1 8 3 9 1 9 2 8 3 8 *